I am my father's son.

SCORCHED
A NEW BEGINNING

USA TODAY BESTSELLING AUTHORS
YOLANDA OLSON
JENNIFER BENE

Text copyright © 2020 Yolanda Olson and Jennifer Bene

All Rights Reserved

No part of this book may be reproduced in any form or by any electronic or mechanical means including information storage and retrieval systems, without permission in writing from the author. The only exception is by a reviewer, who may quote short excerpts in a review.

This book is a work of fiction. Names, characters, places, and incidents either are products of the author's imagination or are used fictitiously. Any resemblance to actual persons, living or dead, events, or locales is entirely coincidental.

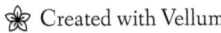 Created with Vellum

Inferno Series by Yolanda Olson

Inferno
Cinere
Sparks
Embers

Inferno World - Volume 1

Verboten by A. A. Davies
Malignus by Dani René
Iniquity by Emery LeeAnn
Burned by Jennifer Bene
Obloquy by Murphy Wallace

Inferno World - Volume 2
Flagrant by Ally Vance
Cognati by Elizabeth Gray
Desiccate by Charity B.
Simmer by Measha Stone

A New Beginning
Scorched by Yolanda Olson & Jennifer Bene

Introduction

I bet you never thought you'd hear from me again, but this ... this is something special.

You know my son Richter, but do you know my other one? Bryden always wanted to live up to the Greene Family name and I wondered if he ever did. If you haven't met my eldest son, you'll find him in 'Burned.' Be careful not to get too burned around him though—I heard he was a real pisser.

I can't say that I'm proud of either of them, I mean how many times can one man fuck up like I did and get it right? I'd have to say none.

Except for Darby.

But we're not here to talk about her, we're here because you've decided that you want to find out who carries on the Greene Family name. You want to see if maybe I *can* feel proud of one of these useless fucking kids for once.

And you know what?

So do I.

Anyway, enough from me.

Go meet my boys and tell them Pater sent you.

Prologue

RICHTER

I use the back of my hand to wipe the excess beer from my lips. I don't know where Skylar is. Unlike our father, I let her have the run of the property because I know that just looking at me sometimes is enough to make her sick.

I get it though since I have enough of a hard time myself looking at my own reflection. It makes me wonder why I fell victim to the affliction that's plagued my family.

Love in the way that my father taught me, as taught to him by his mother—it should be enough to make anyone sick, but I loved my father. I never knew that Mom was really my sister until he explained it to me before he died, and somehow, it didn't matter to me. I didn't think of him as a monster, because in his eyes, I saw a reflection of myself.

A lost soul trying to find love in a world so fucking cold that it's damn near impossible.

I raise the amber bottle to my lips and chuckle slightly.

I loved my mother. It made sense after he sealed her up in the well why she was always sending us outside. Why she was so careful with him when he lost his temper. After Dad locked us up in cages out in the woods, he warned us that if we made even the slightest peep, he'd kill Mom.

And even though we were the perfect, obedient children he always wanted… he killed her anyway.

Was it really her fault like he swore to us that it was? No; I don't believe so, but I knew better than to speak against him. He never knew it, but I would see what he did to her when I would sneak back into the house and wonder why she was crying or shouting.

I once caught him hitting her. I often heard all of the ugly things he would say to her, and I saw him fuck her once or twice.

Still, I found no fault in the way he disciplined her. For a long time after she died, I couldn't help but think that she deserved it for not fighting back more than she did.

That bastard is the Dad in me. However, knowing she did everything she possibly could do to shield us from what she thought was a well-kept family secret makes me wonder if I could have been more of the 'brave boy' she always told me I was.

Maybe I could have saved Mom. Maybe I could have saved all of us.

That would-be hero is the Darby in me.

I'm the imperfect balance of the good I wish to see in the world, and the indifference for life that flows through my veins.

I have to protect my sister.

I have to find the one Dad threw away.

I'll do my best to reunite us all under one roof and make this the perfect family again.

It's what he would have wanted.

Please understand when I tell you that I am *not* a monster.

I *am* simply my father's son.

ONE

Richter

It took a long time for me to figure out the internet since Dad never let us have any kind of contact with the outside world. Lucky for me, when he died, he left me everything he owned.

Dad had lots of antiques that I was able to sell to get some money. His life insurance payout was insanely huge, and that's something I've been trying not to touch. Besides, the less things of his that are in the house, the easier it might be to clean the dirty aura that hangs low over this family.

When Mom was alive, she made friends with the postman. Every time Dad disappeared into town, which was far and few in between, she would sit outside and wait for her friend.

Mr. Hall, I think his name was. I would peek out the window and watch how happy she'd be when he would take a few minutes out of his schedule to sit on the front steps and talk to her. They'd flip through magazines and catalogs while Mom would ask questions and he'd answer them as best as he could.

It's how I found out about computers and the internet.

They were in one of the electronic store flyers that Mr. Hall let Mom have. She hid it from Dad, but she taught the three of us everything she could figure out from the advertisements.

That's why, when the opportunity presented itself, I sold half of the old man's shit and got one.

The first time in town alone was kind of scary. A shellshock, I guess, since I wasn't used to anything other than the walls that housed us for all of our lives. But I did what I had to do.

I don't use it for base entertainment. My main purpose in trying to figure out the entire world inside this expensive, fancy, little box is to try and find Cleo.

That poor kid never really did know up from down, and it broke my heart the day Dad left with her and came back empty handed.

I know he was doing it to punish Mom, but he punished me and Skylar too by taking away our little sister.

And I'm going to make it right.

As I settle down in Dad's old den and power the computer on, I flip open the small notebook that sits next to the mouse. I've been doing my best to keep notes on everything I've found out about where she could be so far, and I hope that I'll be able to pin her location down sooner rather than later.

I miss that little girl.

Not that she would be little at this point, I think in sudden shock. It's been more than ten years since we last saw each other. Another three years have gone by since I've been trying to get Skylar used to us being a family the way Dad would have wanted. That would make Cleo... *eighteen?*

A shudder goes through me as I sit back for a moment in

the realization that my baby sister isn't a baby anymore. It wounds me and fills my soul at the same time.

The pain comes from not being able to see her grow up, but the hope is that she won't be too young for me. I know it will take less convincing with her to understand how our family loves each other, because of all the children Dad had, she was the only one that showed signs of inbreeding.

I always thought she was beautiful in her own way, though. From what I can remember, she has the same eye color as Dad, but the rest belonged to Mom. Her soft-spoken kindness and the way she wanted to make sure everyone was always happy… that was definitely the Darby in all of us.

She always did her best to put on a brave face and smile. She always wanted Mom and Dad to approve of her every move and I guess, in a way, that makes her better than me and Skylar.

I do what I do because it's my birthright. Skylar allows it because she has no fight left in her. Cleo on the other hand? She's a fighter; always has been. I miss her more than I can honestly put into words and I know it's best for her to be back in the family home where she belongs.

TWO

Richter

"Thank you," I say softly as Skylar reappears for the first time today to set a cup of coffee by my notebook.

"You're welcome," she replies quietly. I steal a glance up at her as she crosses her arms over her chest and peers at the screen. "Have you found her yet?"

I shake my head and blow out my breath. "Not any closer than I was yesterday, but I'm trying."

Skylar nods as she settles onto the edge of the desk, a thoughtful look on her face. "I wonder if she's had a good life," she muses softly. "It would be a shame to rip her away from everything she knows to bring her back here, Richter."

"What's so bad about being here?" I shoot back through gritted teeth. *Deep breath; count to ten, don't be like him.*

She scoffs as she pushes herself away from the desk, making her way toward the door. In my heart, I know that Skylar loves me, but in my mind, I wonder if I'm doing this all wrong since she acts more like a goddamn hostage than my supposed wife.

It frustrates me to no end because I try to do the opposite of all the things I saw Dad do when they thought we were outside playing. I don't force myself on Skylar, I try to never hit her or raise my voice to her. I know she loves me. I just want her to love me the way that I love her—the way that Dad loved Mom.

"Skylar?" I call out as I watch her open the door.

She glances at me over her shoulder, lingering in the doorway with an arched eyebrow.

"Aren't you happy here?" I question, a wave of confusion washing over me. This isn't turning out to be anything like Dad said it would. She seems to be sadder, emptier, and even angrier as the days go on.

Skylar bites her lower lip for a moment before dropping her eyes to the floor and walking out of the room, taking any hope of an answer with her.

Am I doing this wrong?

I let out a heavy sigh as I turn my attention back to the screen in front of me, raising the cup of coffee to my lips, and taking a sip of the warm brew.

'She'll be a pain in the ass at first, son. They always fucking are,' he'd said with a tired laugh. 'But she'll come around when she understands that what you're doing is for her own good. No one outside of this family has ever been able to handle a Greene, and I know you'll do me proud in the end.'

And that's all I really want, honestly. To make the old man proud of me—it's all any of his children fucking wanted. As one of the last three standing, I plan on following through with the promise I made him. I'll be the one that makes him proud.

I walk excitedly into the kitchen where Sky is fixing us some lunch, a small pep in my step, and feeling like the best brother in the world. She'll be so happy to know that I finally got a good lead on where our little sister might be, and that I want her to go into town with me to see if we can find her.

Dad always left us behind, but that's not the kind of husband I want to be. I want us to be together all the time—even though I know it's a burden to be around someone who loves as deeply as I do, I just hate the thought of being apart from my sisters for longer than I have to be.

And I've been away from Cleo for far too long—we both have.

"Guess what, Sky?" I ask when I enter the kitchen. She glances at me quickly to let me know that I have her attention, and as I reach into the fridge for a bottle of beer, I suddenly find myself wondering if she'll be as happy as I am about the 'good news.'

After all, she *did* say that Cleo might be better off wherever she is, but I don't think she really believes that.

"Well," I press with a nervous laugh. "Guess!"

She clears her throat and turns to face me, one hand still stirring the pot on the stove while the other finds its place on her hip. I remember times when Mom used to look at us like that. She would always ask us to tell her stories of what we would do outside, but she told us to make things up. Not to lie to her per se, but to encourage us to make up worlds outside of the only life we knew.

And she would stand just like the way Sky is standing now.

"I don't know," she finally replies quietly.

I do my best not to let my face crumple into a mask of disappointment. The way she is now—the bitterness, the resentment, the doing her best to make sure she doesn't end up in bed with me—it's my fault for not knowing how to do this right.

There are some days where I wish that Dad was still alive. He'd be able to show me, and I learn things easier if I can see them instead of being told.

I guess it's why I never really did well when Mom would quiz us on our studies, I think with a rueful smile.

But I decide that if I keep the mood in the kitchen as upbeat as I felt when I found the information I was looking for, then maybe she'll share in my excitement too.

"I think I found our little sister."

THREE

Bryden
———————

This house runs so much smoother than it did years ago. Back when I still had Marian here, and Ella, and Wesley. I never hated them, I never really wanted to be without them —but a family is such a precious thing. It's delicate, sensitive, and... well, they just stopped trying.

Having a good family, a loving, happy family, takes work. I've always been the one willing to put in that work, and it's my love that has carried each and every one of my children over the years.

I built this family out of the wreckage of mine and Marian's histories, I keep this family on course, and it's been worth every single trial and tribulation.

Even though Ella and Wesley were never the same after the day their mama died, Ella still gave me three beautiful children. Two girls, Tristan and my Xoe, and then Damon. He'd been a sweet boy until he just stopped trying too. But Tristan... she'd been tainted by her mama. Too old the day Wesley decided to finally try and unseat me as head of this family—but he'd failed. I'd always known he would, and I'd secretly hoped each night that he'd wait a little longer to try and ruin our growing family. Twenty-one was too young to get put in the ground.

And after her brother was gone, Ella had just fallen apart. I'd caught her whispering terrible things to Tristan, to *my* little girl. The chain and the closet obviously hadn't been enough of a punishment to remind her of my rules, my expectations, because then she'd come at me too. Woke me up with a knife to my throat, so much like her mama, and she'd gone out the same way. Sweetly, gently, with my hands around her throat. With me reminding her that I loved her but that I wouldn't let her ruin our family. It was simply time for her to go and be with her brother and mama.

But I know it was the shit she whispered to Tristan that made the girl eventually rebel. She never came to my room joyfully, and I don't think she ever loved our children—not really. But I'd hoped she'd understand some day. I'd given her so many chances, but when I found her packing a bag for the two she'd birthed... well, she had to go in the ground too. Buried right next to her mama, and maybe her father too. I never stressed much over whether it was me or Wesley who put those seeds in Ella's belly, because Wesley was my blood too.

But Xoe.

My sweet Xoe.

She is definitely mine. Marian's blonde hair, but my eyes, my spirit, my complete dedication to keeping this family together. She loves me more than Marian was ever capable, more than Ella ever tried to. It was good that I let Ella go when I did, because she never had the chance to taint Xoe, and Xoe loves me the most.

I love her too, but I have to remind myself never to play

favorites. Never to let one of my children feel alone, feel disregarded, unloved.

There are times I still blame myself for how Damon turned out. Xoe wanted so much of my time, she came to my bed as often as she could... and I let her. I didn't make enough time for Damon. I didn't love them equally. No, I let him wander, and I let him down. He loved Tristan, his oldest sister, and when she was gone... I lost him even more. It was a mercy to put him in the ground beside her. To let them be together so that our family could thrive—and we *are* thriving now.

They are all so beautiful.

So loved.

I hear someone shout and it pulls me from my memories. Someone else starts crying, and I set my coffee cup down to shade my eyes and look out across the field behind the house. Embry is the one crying, and Owen is looking guilty as hell. But before I can even stand up, Heather is already turning around to scoop Embry up in her arms and I can't help but smile as she perches the girl on her hip and coos at her before she leans down to talk to Owen. I know he's apologizing to his sister like a good boy, but he's only seven and I've raised too many kids to be worried about it.

There are days I wonder if Marian would have liked to have seen this. So many kids running around, each and every one of them knowing how loved they are. Safe. Shielded from the terrible world outside our little slice of paradise.

But then I remember how jealous she would get. I remember her pulling a knife on me, and I'm not sorry in the least that she missed her chance to see our blood continue. That selfish traitor doesn't deserve to know the shining faces that overflow our house.

Even after I built on an extra room so the girls could spread out, we're still packed in, but it's nice. Pretty damn warm in the winter cold. The living room converts at night to a bedroom for the little ones, and everyone is happy together. The older kids have the bedrooms, the little ones have their cribs lining the walls in the living room, and there's always a fire going in the winter.

Damon helped me build those cribs, and even though he's not with us anymore, his touch is on every spindle of wood. He'd had a talent for it, and it's a shame he couldn't have been more like Xoe. More committed to working hard, being good.

But boys are always different.

"Hey Daddy," Casey says as he walks outside to stand next to me. He has oil on his hands and the sleeves of his pullover, and I know he's been working on the car. It's a piece of junk, but Casey has a way with machines. Taught himself from manuals I picked up for him in town. He leans down and pecks me on the lips before he glances out over the younger kids. Any of them could be mine, or his, but just like Wesley I've never felt jealous over that. Casey is my blood, and so they all are. "Who was wailing? I heard it out front."

"Embry," I answer with a smile. "I think Owen got a little frustrated that his little sister wanted to play with him."

"He knows better than to be mean to her," Casey replies with a hard edge to his voice, and I nod as I watch the kids return to making snowballs. Laughing as they jump into the white powder and start to make snow angels, and this time Owen and Gavin are letting Embry do it too.

"They're having fun now, it's all right."

Casey nods and grabs the chair on the other side of the little table. He tries his best to wipe his hands on the rag in his pocket before he pours himself a glass of iced tea, and just looking at him makes me smile. Casey may be Tristan's son, but he doesn't have her rebellious nature. Not at all. Even when he was Owen's age, he was the protector. Shepherding his sisters around, watching out for them, and for once I think I might have finally gotten it right with a boy.

Casey reminds me of me. Eager to show his love, committed to what is right. He wants to be just like me when he grows up, and since he's already nineteen and hasn't once defied me... I think I might let him see what he's capable of.

FOUR

Richter

Sky has an eyebrow arched. She's looking at me almost as if she's not sure whether to believe me, but I wouldn't lie about something like this.

"Did you hear what I said?" I ask, nervously rubbing the back of my neck.

She nods, then turns her attention back to lunch, but I'm not interested in eating right now. I'm interested in sharing the information I found with her—whether she wants it or not.

"I couldn't sleep last night so I went into the old man's room," I begin, trying to keep the frustration out of my tone. When she steals a glance at me, I smile and shrug. "I know. We promised that we wouldn't go back in there, but sometimes it still smells like him in there. Mom too," I say softly. It's almost a confession spilling out of me. We keep the door locked at all times because we don't want to relive the memory of Dad being here if we don't have to, but sometimes... I just need to remember that Mom was here too.

"It's okay," she says quietly. Skylar does her best to convince me that everything wrong I do is okay, and I let her think she has. It's the only way we'll be able to make it through any of this together.

"Thanks," I mumble before I clear my throat and try to straighten my shoulders. "Anyway, I was looking through his stuff and I found some birth records. Who would have thought he actually kept those or that he had someone help Mom give birth, you know? The point is, I used the info on Cleo's birth certificate online and I think I know where she is now."

"How did you do that?" Sky asks, finally turning back toward me and handing me a small bowl. I glance down and use the fork inside to stab some of the lettuce, one of the small tomatoes, and a long string of cheese, then shovel it into my mouth. I chew thoughtfully for a moment, assuming the pot on the stove is for dinner and wondering how the hell a salad could have taken so long—but then I remember that she makes do with what we have, and I should appreciate that she cares enough to throw something together for me too.

"Well, don't get mad, alright?" I begin a little sheepishly. When she nods in agreement, I grin proudly. "I've been watching videos on how to hack into websites and stuff and I broke into the database for Social Services. Before you get mad, I used a VPN or whatever it's called, and they won't know I was there. I didn't change anything; I just got an address and left."

"Is that what you do in that damn den all day?" she snaps at me. "Figure out ways to break the law from the comfort of your own home?"

The grin immediately leaves my face. I place the bowl

down on the counter, a rage starting to rise inside of me, and I have to remind myself that I'm not Dad.

I'm *not*.

Sky doesn't look the least bit worried when I start closing the small amount of space between us. She doesn't even flinch when I raise my hand, but when I close my fist and strike her across the face with it, she drops to the floor and looks up at me in shock with a split lip.

Okay.

I'm not Dad.

I guess I'm worse.

"I'm sorry, Sky," I tell her for what seems like the fifteenth time in half an hour. "I promise I'll never do that again. I shouldn't have done it to begin with! Forgive me? Please?"

I know I sound like a needy little boy right now, but with as many times as I saw Dad raise his hand to Mom, I should have known better. I should have been able to control my fucking temper.

It's just... the smell of him. It brings me back to the time he was still here—and it makes me angry all over again.

I let out a long-suffering sigh as I get to my feet and decide that I should go to the address I found alone and just see if Cleo's even there.

"I'll be back in a couple of hours," I tell her softly. She has her arms firmly crossed over her chest and refuses to meet my eyes. It means that I'll have to make sure all the windows and doors are padlocked before I leave, because I know Sky and she'll try to run away if she's not locked in.

After spending the next thirty minutes making sure that Skylar will be safely secured while I'm gone, I walk into the den and grab the scrap of paper I scribbled the information on.

Bryden Furay, huh? Let's see if you have my little sister, I think as I lock the door to the den and make my way toward the front door.

FIVE

Xoe

Something crashes in the living room and I lean back from the stove to look at the chaos of my family, but I don't hear shouting or crying so I'm not that worried.

"I can finish up if you want to get Daddy," Brinnah says, wiping her hands on a towel as she waits patiently beside me. Of all my girls, she's the closest to me, and she's always trying to help. Although none of the children fail to help when needed, they all know when it's time to work, and I love them all for it.

Pressing a kiss to Brinnah's forehead, I smile down at her. "Thanks, honey. I'll go see if Daddy is ready to eat."

Walking through the living room is an act of dexterity. The little ones have toys scattered everywhere, and I know exactly what crashed before. There are wooden blocks in a massive pile, and I can tell from the guilty glance I get from Gavin that he's responsible.

"Did you knock this down?" I ask, holding onto my smile so he knows he's not in trouble.

"Yes, mama," Gavin answers, and he's already sitting down to pick them up.

"Let's get the living room neat before Daddy says it's time for lunch, okay?" I give him a gentle squeeze on the shoulder before I head back to Daddy's bedroom. Gavin is ten, but I can already tell he's going to be just as responsible as Casey is, and I'm grateful for that. If there's one thing that Daddy doesn't tolerate, it's laziness.

But betrayal is worse.

That thought makes my stomach turn because it makes me remember my siblings. They both had to go away because they wanted to hurt our family, and I've never faulted Daddy for that—but I still miss them sometimes. I can still see Tristan in Casey's eyes though, and in the way Sierra laughs when she plays a game with Cleo.

I'm pretty sure that my brother Damon fathered Moira, my second girl, but that's only because she has his dimples... and she's a dreamer like he was.

Yeah, she reminds me of Damon on his best days.

As I knock on the door of Daddy's room, I listen to the sounds inside and smile. Heather is just like me. My first, my ray of sunshine, and she loves Daddy as much as I do.

"Daddy?" I call through the door and wait.

"Come in, Xoe!" he calls back with a grunt, and I open the door to see Heather on top of him, rocking back and forth as she seeks her pleasure and his. I couldn't be more proud, and they both smile at me as Daddy squeezes her hips.

Closing the door behind me, I stand just inside, watching as they continue to love each other. Heather already has two children, but I know she wants more, and she finds times like this to love her Daddy.

"Do you need me, Mama?" she asks, breathy, whining through her teeth as he thrusts hard, and my own body clenches with need.

I'll be seeking his bed tonight, I promise myself.

"No, honey, just checking with Daddy to see when he'd like us to serve lunch."

His eyes are closed, lost to the act of love as Heather braces her hands on his shoulders and starts to move just like I taught her. A second later she's moaning, shuddering, and Daddy rolls them so she can enjoy the pleasure she's earned as he works to finish. I can't help but stare at the strong planes of Daddy's back, the way his muscles move under his skin, and my own need ratchets up—but I'll wait.

I've always been patient for my time with Daddy, and he's given me five beautiful children for it.

Possibly six, but we won't know that for another month or so.

He groans and I squeeze my thighs together as I watch him lean down to kiss Heather, whispering how much he loves her, and she says it back.

We all love each other, and that's all Daddy has ever wanted... and now he has it.

I know how hard he worked to build our family, everything he's done for us, and it's just one more reason why I love him more than anything else in the world.

The moment he moves to lie beside Heather, he reaches out his hand for me, and I can't resist the urge to join them.

"Brinnah is finishing lunch," I remind him as I crawl onto the bed to lie beside him, resting my head on his shoulder, and his arm curls around me.

"My girls," he whispers, pressing a kiss to my hair before turning to do the same to Heather. "I love you both so much."

"I love you, too," I reply at the same time as Heather, and we smile at each other.

"Heather, I want to talk to your mama real quick, will

you help your sister finish lunch? We'll be out soon." Daddy gives her another kiss, and then she hops out of bed.

"Okay, Daddy," she answers as she walks to the door and slips the dress over her head, tugging her underwear back on. "Love you, Mama!"

Heather waves as she walks out of the room, closing the door behind her, and I turn back to Daddy to wait for him to speak. It's never helpful to rush him, he likes to think things through before he talks to us, and it means I can run my hand over his chest. Touching him, just us, and it's a moment we don't always get to steal during the day.

He may be older, but his body is strong. All the work he's done on the house and the property has kept him healthy, and I'm grateful for it. If he went into the ground, I don't know how any of us would survive the loss.

"You know how much I love you, and Heather, right?" he asks, and I nod. His warm smile crosses his mouth before he leans down to kiss me, our tongues brushing for a moment. "Mmm... see, this is what I'm talking about. I need you girls to share. I love all of you equally, and it's hard to do that when you and Heather seek my love so often."

I can't hide the pain in my expression from him, he always knows what I'm thinking, but this time I don't even want to. I'd had my heart set on being in his bed tonight.

"Xoe, you know I love you so much. You've helped me keep this family happy and growing, and I will never let you feel alone." Daddy touches my cheek and I nod slowly.

"But you don't want anyone to feel unloved," I fill in the blanks of what he's trying to say, and I can't even deny that between Heather and I we monopolize too much of his time.

"That's right, and I need you to help me with that. Speak to Heather about it. I wanted to, but I'd never want to hurt her feelings, and she'll understand better if it comes from you." Another kiss to my lips as he pauses. "How would you have felt if I never had time for you?"

That question pricks a place deep inside me, one that makes me feel guilt for denying anyone in our family his love.

"I'm sorry, Daddy," I whisper through the threatening edge of tears.

"No, no, Xoe." He shushes me as he squeezes me closer to him. "Things are just changing as there are more of us, that's all. I still love all of you equally, and that will never change."

"I know, Daddy."

"Good girl," he replies, and it makes me feel like I'm glowing as he kisses me again. The tears are gone before he pulls away, and I smile. "Go on and get everyone to the table, I'll get cleaned up and be out soon."

"I will, I promise." I steal one more kiss before I climb out of bed, and he chuckles as he stands up. He stretches in the light from the window, and I soak in the sight of him before I make myself walk out of his room.

Peeking into the living room, I spy Casey in Daddy's chair and I wave to get his attention. "Can you get everyone to the table? I'm going to get the girls."

"Yes, ma'am," he answers fast, closing the book in his lap before he stands up, snagging a wiggling Abigail — the youngest — before he winks at me. "I've got it."

"Thank you, Casey." I walk to the end of the hall and open the door to their room, finding the girls exactly where I expected them to be on this cold day. Hidden under a blanket fort in the corner between two of the beds.

Shifting to my knees, I crawl to the edge of their

hideaway and whisper, "Is there anyone in this noble castle that may want some lunch?"

Cleo's head peeks out between two blankets, her brown hair is in her face, tangled, and I reach forward to tuck the majority of it behind her ears.

She scrunches up her nose at me, and I smile at her. "Would you like to have some lunch?"

"I guess so," she answers, and then her eyes widen a bit. "Wait."

She tucks herself back inside the fort, and I sit down as I hear her and Sierra whispering away.

This time, Sierra peeks her head out. "Is anyone in trouble?"

"Nope." I shake my head as Cleo's face breaks through the blankets right beside Sierra's. Smiling indulgently at my special girls, because I know it's better to let them come out on their own, I stand up. "Daddy is about to come to the table, so if you want to get a good seat you should hurry up and escape your castle!"

Giggles start up at my back as I walk to the door and head back to the kitchen. Heather and Brinnah are putting dishes on the tables, and Casey is busy wrangling the younger ones with Moira's help. I just stand in the doorway and watch as the two tables start to fill up with our family.

Somedays it's hard to believe that our big family is so perfect, and I know that the hard decisions Daddy had to make about my mama—and my siblings—were worth it. We'd never be this happy with their destructive tendencies in our home.

I feel arms slide around my waist just before Daddy hugs me back against his chest, and I know he's looking at everyone as they find seats. The older ones propping the little ones on their laps, and Daddy's seat at the head of the table is empty, and the one to his right is waiting for me.

"I love you, Xoe," he whispers against my ear, just before he nips my neck in a way that sends tingles down my spine.

"I love you so much, Daddy," I reply softly just as Cleo and Sierra flit past us to find their seats. I'm proud when I watch Owen move seats so the two girls can sit next to each other—it's just one more way they show that they love each other.

And that's what our house is... full of love.

Thanks to Daddy.

"Ready?" I ask, and he squeezes me tight before he lets go and guides us to our seats.

The chorus of "Hi, Daddy" around the table has him laughing, and he smiles big as he pulls his chair in.

"We've had such a good morning. Let's all thank those that helped make lunch for us."

Thank yous, pop up around the room, and I nod my head with a smile, looking around at everyone.

Daddy reaches for the food and puts the first serving on his plate, and everyone waits for him to finish like we're supposed to. He leans over to squeeze my knee, and then he nods at everyone. "Let's eat!"

SIX

Richter

The one thing the old man always taught us when we were kids was to never talk to strangers. Mom broke that rule of his when she started chatting up the mailman, but they became friends after a while, and I'd like to think that maybe there are other people as kind as he was to her outside the walls of our house.

Not that there's time to worry about that.

Not that there's time to worry about much of anything that isn't bringing my baby sister home and being a family again.

I try not to think of what Sky said, that Cleo might be happier in the life she has now than one with us because that's not what Dad would have wanted.

I saw the way he would look at her. Sometimes it was disgust, sometimes it was sadness, but no matter what he said, or how he treated *any* of us, I know that old man loved us. I know it.

If he didn't, we wouldn't have found out how a family is supposed to work.

I grunt as I reach the end of our driveway wondering

which direction to go to get to this Bryden Furay's house. I'm a little agitated now because I don't really know my way around.

Follow your heart, kid; you'll always find your family that way.

With a sigh, and a silent thanks to Dad, I decide to turn right and start making my way to town. Someone there will know which way I need to go, and maybe they'll be as nice as the mailman.

Even if Cleo isn't there anymore, there's still a small flicker of hope in me that this man can point me in the right direction.

An extra step in the quest for finding my baby sister and hopefully reuniting with her. I wonder who she looks like now. As a child, she was the perfect mix of Mom and Dad, but she leaned slightly more toward Mom. It was like watching an altered, confused little clone of Mom with Dad's temper and swagger running around in the backyard.

Sometimes, I would see his anger in her eyes when she didn't quite understand something, but I was always able to calm her down. Sky helped too, but not much—she was far too interested in being a princess and was Daddy's Little Snitch more than she cared to admit.

Because of that, I didn't share as much with Sky as I did with Cleo. Partly because I didn't want to get tattled on, and partly because I knew Cleo wouldn't really get what I was saying anyway. She was great for venting to since she would just sit there and watch me with confused eyes and a hopeful smile.

It wasn't her fault that she didn't understand a lot of things, but it wasn't Mom or Dad's fault either. I think sometimes things happen for a reason and Cleo got the short end of the stick.

I never loved her any less for being different, and I like to think that Sky didn't either.

I ease the truck to the stop sign at the edge of town and sigh heavily. *Left, right, or onward?* My heart tells me to continue in a straight line and I'll find what I'm looking for, so when it's my turn to continue, I gently press down on the gas pedal and continue on my way.

I'm sitting inside my truck, chewing the inside of my mouth thoughtfully. It seems that I have the right address from what I've written down, but I'm not entirely sure what to say.

Hi, my name is Richter Greene and I'm looking for my little sister, Cleo. Have you seen her?

I scratch my head, deciding that the direct approach is probably best, and undo my seatbelt. I check the rearview mirror before stepping out of my truck and slide my keys into my pocket.

One last deep breath, a look down either way of the long, country road, and I start walking up the dirt drive.

I smile at the size of the house.

It's not huge, but it's almost as big as the one I lived in with Cleo, except it's only one story.

Hopefully I'm not disturbing anyone, I think nervously.

After I make my way up the walkway, I raise a hand and knock on the door, waiting patiently for someone to acknowledge that I'm here.

A few minutes pass and there's still no sign of life inside, even though I can hear conversation, so I knock again, a little louder this time. And that's enough to send a set of footsteps quickly toward the front door. I can hear the faint echoing from inside, becoming louder and clearer the closer they get.

The door opens slightly and a beautiful woman with blonde hair peeks out at me.

"Can I help you?" she asks curiously.

"Um," I stammer. I can't help it—she's fucking gorgeous. With a friendly smile, she leans her head against the door frame, waiting patiently for me to regain my bearings.

"I can't help you if I don't know what you need," she remarks in a curious, but friendly tone.

"Oh, sorry," I reply, my face blushing crimson red. "I was looking for—" I fish the piece of scrap paper out of my hand, glance down at the name, then look back into her eyes. "Bryden Furay."

"Daddy!" she calls back over her shoulder.

I smile nervously and scuff my shoe against the porch while I wait. A few moments later, I'm greeted by an older man—one with eyes that seem so fucking familiar that I narrow mine as I inspect him.

"I'm Bryden, how can I help you?" he asks, stepping out and extending his hand.

The smell of him is so familiar.

The way his touch feels when I take his hand in mine makes me nervous.

But his eyes.

The longer I look into his eyes, the more I'm starting to wonder... because the eyes that are staring back at me are unique. They're almost like the blonde girl's that opened the door for me, but in that masculine frame of a face...

There's no way—he would have told us.

"I'm Richter Greene. I'm looking for my sister Cleo."

Bryden raises an eyebrow as his hand tightens around mine and he gives me a gentle jerk toward him.

"What did you say your name was?" he asks in a hushed tone.

"Richter."

"Your last name," he says in a stern tone with a shake of his head. "What's your last name?"

"Greene," I reply nervously, taking a step back and wrenching my hand out of his grip.

He looks me up and down, narrows his eyes, and shakes his head.

"That bastard," he mumbles under his breath. "That goddamn bastard."

SEVEN

Bryden

"Come in," I say as I step back from the door. My head is spinning as the young man walks inside my home, his eyes going directly to the little ones playing on the living room floor, and I close the door slowly to give myself time to think.

Richter Greene.

GREENE. Like the ink on my back. The name I worked a lifetime to earn... and even after I'd proven I was a Greene; it wasn't enough for him to tell me *this* in person? Not enough to know about the young man who shares my blood?

Luke's blood.

Our blood.

I take a deep breath, trying to be as welcoming as I should be to family while I think through Luke's reasoning for keeping Richter from me.

"Let's talk in the kitchen," I suggest, leading him that way as his head continues to swivel. It makes me smile because he looks wide-eyed. A little overwhelmed, maybe a bit impressed, and I can't help but feel pride as I watch

Heather helping our girl Embry write the alphabet on the floor.

The chaos of the house keeps distracting him as I take my seat at the head of the table, and he hesitates in the doorway as Gavin and Owen come racing through the living room in their coats. They're out the door too fast, laughing, and I hear Casey remind them about the backdoor as he shuts it.

"This is your family?" he asks, and I wait for him to return his gaze to mine before I nod.

"It is, and... apparently so are you." I let the statement rest there for a moment as his brow furrows and he lowers himself into the chair on my left.

"We're..."

"Family," I finish for him. "It's nice to meet you."

Richter still looks dazed, and I feel for him. I'm still processing the idea too, still feeling the hurt of Luke keeping one more thing from me for so long—but I think it's the house full of kids that's really got him so distracted.

"Let's clear the air, Richter. Who is your father?" I ask, just to be sure. He'd called Cleo his sister, but that wasn't a guarantee.

"Luke Greene," he answers, and I have to admit it hurts. I manage another nod, forcing a smile onto my face again as I lean back in the chair.

"Well, then... I guess we're brothers, Richter. I'm always glad to have more family in my life, and I'm happy you came to find me."

"That's not possible." Richter frowns for a second and shakes his head. "He would have told me about you, and I didn't come here to find *you*. I came here to find Cleo and bring her home."

"Well, he didn't tell me about you either," I reply with a chuckle, ignoring his second mention of Cleo for now.

"Who was your mom?" Richter asks, sitting up straight in the chair, and I can tell he's trying to look bigger.

"A woman named Sheila," I answer, spreading my hands. "I don't keep secrets in my house, Richter. You can ask me anything you like."

I respect the fact that he doesn't immediately ask a question. He waits, thinks, and I can see Luke in his expression... but there's something softer to it. Maybe it's the way his eyes keep returning to my face, judging but curious. He doesn't believe me yet, but he will.

Family always knows family.

He shakes his head and meets my gaze again, voice harder this time. "I just want to know if you have Cleo or not."

Hmm.

It's my turn to appraise him, to weigh how to answer, because I'm sure that I know secrets that Richter doesn't. After all, he didn't know about me, so why would he know how she came to be a part of my family?

Luke brought Cleo to my house thirteen years ago, and I'd been stunned to know he had another daughter. Even more surprised to see that she was the same age as my own kids—and he'd never mentioned her once. Not on any visit to my house where he'd shared his love with Tristan and Xoe. Not a single goddamn mention of the little girl until she was in his arms on my front porch.

He'd kept so many secrets, but on that day Luke had entrusted me with Cleo. Given me the gift of his own child, *his blood*, to be raised in my house. And with her had finally come the acknowledgement that I was his blood too.

His son.

His first born.

It was all I'd ever wanted, but he'd never mentioned another child as he stood on my front porch. Never spoke of a son as Cleo cried and reached for him while I tried to comfort her.

He'd left that day and never came back.

Why share your secrets now, Luke?

"So..." I clear my throat and brush some dust off the kitchen table. "Luke told you where Cleo was?"

"No, I found her online. Through Social Services. You received benefits for her at this address."

"Ah." I nod and look at him, feeling the stern edge slip into my voice. "Does your father know you're here?"

"No." Richter shakes his head. "He died... ten years ago now."

The whole world tilts and I find my fingers have a white-knuckle grip on the edge of the table as those words whirl in my head.

Dead? Luke is dead?

"What?" I ask on a ragged breath, because it feels like my ears are buzzing and I'm sure I didn't hear him correctly.

"Dad died a long time ago," Richter replies, and he leans forward. "You didn't know?"

Shaking my head, I try not to let the uneasy feeling in my bones show on my face, but I know I'm failing. It's impossible to think about, impossible to be true. Luke was... constant. He may have looked older in those years when he reached out again, came to meet my family, to see the legacy I'd built—but dead? Just a few years after he brought Cleo to my door?

It hurts worse than the fact that he kept Richter from me.

My father is gone, and I'd only ever heard him call me 'son' once... but now that memory means so much more.

And Cleo was his last gift to me.

I swallow the lump in my throat, surprised by the swell of emotion I feel, but now I know it's even more important that Richter found me, found *us*.

"Who have you been living with?" I ask, and he just stares at me, so I rephrase the question. "I mean, is your mother still there?"

"No, she died too. Before dad."

"You've been alone all this time?" The thought makes me want to pull him into a hug, to let him know he's loved, but he doesn't know me well enough yet—and he's not mine.

At least, not until he chooses it.

"No... I've been with Skylar. My other sister." The words roll off his tongue so easily, and I'm still so stunned by everything else the boy has shared that the reality of another child isn't as much of a shock.

Actually, the absurdity of it all has me laughing under my breath as I shake my head.

"I loved Luke, you know? I really did... but goddamn he could be a bastard." Reaching across the table, I pat Richter's arm. "Don't worry though, you're welcome here. We're family, and that's all that matters."

"Thanks," Richter mumbles, twisting in his chair to look back at the living room, surveying the house, and I know he's looking for Cleo—but he won't find her. She'll be tucked away somewhere with Sierra, and if the boy thinks I'm just handing over one of my children... he's going to be very disappointed.

Then Xoe starts walking toward the kitchen and Richter's eyes are only on her. My girl is beautiful, blonde hair like Marian's, curves that always make my cock twitch, and I can tell Richter sees it too.

"Hi Daddy," she says, stopping next to me to lean down and kiss me on the lips.

"Hi baby." I push my chair back a bit and pull her onto my lap. It's the perfect opportunity to let Richter see how things work here, to help him understand why we should all be together. Smiling at Richter, I tilt my head toward her. "This is Xoe."

"Hi Xoe," he says quietly, and I feel my smile stretch.

"Hi," she answers, and I can tell she's curious about him.

We don't have visitors. Not way out here, so far from town, and even if we did Xoe knows I'd never let anyone near my family. I debate what to tell her but settle on the truth.

No secrets.

"Richter is part of our family, Xoe. We had the same father."

She looks at me, wide brown eyes on mine for a moment before she looks back at Richter and her smile goes radiant. "That's wonderful!"

Xoe stands quickly, leaning forward to hug him tight before pressing a kiss to his cheek. Richter barely has time to lift one arm to brush her back, and then she's back on my lap, bouncing a little from her excitement.

"Everyone is going to be so excited to meet him!" she cheers, turning to hug me too.

"I know, it's quite the surprising gift," I reply as I hug her back, keeping my eyes on Richter. He's got a look of raw need on his face that I know I wore for years—but I won't shut him out of this family.

I'd never do that.

I'm not Luke, I'm better.

And with our father gone, Richter's lucky he found me, found our family. We'll make sure he, and his sister, feel loved. Accepted. Wanted.

That's just what family does.

EIGHT

Skylar

Richter's been gone for longer than he normally is, and while I know I should be more worried than I am, it's just nice to have the house to myself for once.

He probably thinks he's some kind of conquering hero—that bringing Cleo back to this hellhole will make her feel better, but she probably doesn't even know who we are anymore.

I've told him this each time he's brought up locating her, but he doesn't seem to hear me.

'*She belongs with us, Sky. With people that love and understand her.*'

I think he wants to believe it more than anything else because he misses her. He misses the three of us being together in this house, but things are different now.

Mom's dead.

Dad's dead.

And in a way, I'm dead too.

I sometimes wonder if how I feel when my brother is on top of me is the way Mom felt when her father—*our* father—was on top of her too.

Darby was a strong woman.

She tried her best to hide her tears from us. She tried to make sure that we never saw what she endured, and she did her best to make sure that Dad never laid a hand on us the way he did with her.

Oddly enough, even though it broke her heart, I'm sure she was relieved somewhat when he took Cleo away.

My poor baby sister, I think with a shuddering sigh. I loved her with all of my heart, and I still do, but bringing her back to this place of unspeakable horror won't help her.

She doesn't need to dwell in the memories that haunt these hallways. She doesn't deserve to step foot into rooms that will choke her with the hate that lingers in the air.

Richter has done his best to make sure that the memory of Dad isn't exactly well kept, but there are some things that even he can't part with.

Dad's room for instance.

After he died, after the first time my brother touched me, I wanted to break the door down and destroy Dad's bed. After all, it's in that fucking bed that all of this hatred started, because for all of his fatherly fodder, I know that man hated us all.

I don't think he ever told anyone other than Darby that he loved them, and I think she believed him.

That's why she failed.

She allowed herself to believe the lies, to be sucked into his web of bullshit, and in the end, those same meticulously woven threads of silk were what ultimately consumed her in the end.

But Richter isn't hateful like Dad.

He's almost never forced me to do anything I wasn't somewhat willing to submit to, and he usually stops when I beg him to. The throb on my lip was just him losing his temper, losing that internal battle with the side of him that is Dad, because I can push him just like Mom used to with Dad.

But all the things that Dad never was, Richter has a handle on, and all of the things he tried to be, Richter sees as a lesson.

The conundrum is that I love my brother, even if not in the way he hopes for. Though, truth be told, I don't think he understands the different ways a person can show love.

He does as he was taught to do—as Dad was taught to do by his own mother—and he thinks it's okay.

I understand why, even though I can't forgive him for it.

I pull back the curtain in the room I share with him from time to time and glance toward the side of the house.

The oubliette stares back with no eyes. It watches with no life, and it waits with no hope.

I wonder how many Greene women have found their end at the bottom of that abyss besides Darby. Did her mother succumb to that hell too? Did Dad force her into the darkness and forget about her like he did with Mom?

Am I next? I wonder with a soft sigh. *If my end is to come at the bottom of the well, then I hope it comes soon.*

I open my eyes with a start.

I didn't realize how tired I was it seems. I use the palms of my hands to push myself up to a seated position and gently roll my neck on my shoulders from left to right.

After blinking rapidly a few times, I manage to get to my feet and startle when I realize that the sun is going down.

I pull the curtain aside and give the oubliette one more

glance, before I let the fabric swing lazily as I walk out of the room.

Richter should be home by now, and if his hunch was right, he should have our sister with him.

He's much too stubborn to have left her where he found her. Consequences be damned. *Just like Dad,* I think with a tired chuckle as I walk down the hallway then descend the stairs.

After Dad died, Richter opened the room across the hall from his. It's the same space we share on the nights when he thinks he's more to me than he really is, but I think it's predominantly because he feels closer to Dad this way.

With all of the things we witnessed, and all of the bullshit we suffered, he still wants to be close to him.

I sigh heavily as I reach the bottom step and make my way into the living room, expecting to find my family.

Instead, I find it void of another living thing and raise an eyebrow curiously.

Maybe they're in the kitchen.

It wouldn't surprise me if he wanted to feed her when they got home, and not knowing how Cleo is these days, they're probably still sitting in there having as best a conversation as they can.

I glance into the dining room on the way to the kitchen and shrug when I see that it's empty too. I've always been pretty good at guessing games so I'm sure I'm right with where they are.

But...

I'm wrong.

When I walk into the kitchen, it's empty.

The lights are still off, and it seems colder for some reason. Lonelier. Less welcoming. Unloving.

All of the things I associate with Dad.

I wrap my arms around myself and purse my lips.

There's nowhere else in this place that Richter would be. I know this because Dad's bedroom door was closed when I walked out of our room, which means he isn't home.

Has he abandoned me?

Maybe he got tired of all my bitching.

Maybe he found Cleo and decided that they'd be better off without me.

Maybe I should count my blessings... but in a place where hope never lived, those are few and far in between.

So, I do the only thing I can do.

I sit on the kitchen floor with the light still off, rest my head against my knees, and begin to cry.

Greene women never were worth much if another one was around, and maybe Richter is his father's son after all.

I'm sorry, Cleo.

NINE

Bryden

"Let me show you around," I tell Richter, patting Xoe on the ass to make her stand.

He's watching me carefully, and there's so much of Luke in his gaze when I get up as well. Scrutinizing, planning, but he's still just a kid. Richter needs guidance, and I'm more than happy to show him the ropes.

I offer him my hand, but he rebuffs it and stands on his own. Smiling, I gesture ahead of me into the living room and he walks in with Xoe. The little ones are still on the floor, playing with Heather, and she looks up at me with a smile. "Hi Daddy."

"Heather, this is Richter. He's my brother."

Her eyes go wide as she looks at him, pulling Embry onto her lap and away from the pencil and paper in front of them. She's been teaching Embry her letters, and for a moment I remember Stephanie doing the same for me.

"Nice to meet you, Heather," Richter says, almost too quietly, and I want to take his shoulder in my hand and remind him to speak up—but that would be too forward. I need to give him time to warm up.

"So... you're my... uncle?" she asks, her mouth twisting around the word.

"You can just call him Richter, sweetheart," I reply, and she shrugs, accepting it because I've said it. I point at the beautiful three-year-old in her arms. "And this little one is Embry."

"She's mine," Heather says, and then looks up at me with a flicker of panic. "I mean, I'm her mama, but we love everyone equally. We all take turns taking care of the little ones."

"That's right," I say, offering Heather a smile so she knows I'm not upset. Possessiveness is something I don't tolerate in my house, and she knows it, but I know she was just trying to be helpful.

Richter nods, staying silent as his eyes drift to the two younger kids playing in a crib against one wall.

"That's Lissa and Abigail, and... where's Weston?" I ask, glancing around the living room.

"I've got him, Daddy!" Moira calls out as she comes from the hallway, holding the rambunctious boy on her hip. "He just needed a change, didn't you? *Didn't you?*"

She's tickling him and he's giggling with that perfect joy that toddlers have about everything in life. Leaning over, I press a kiss to Weston's head, ruffling his dark hair, and he scrunches up his face at me as he twists away. "No!"

I laugh, and Moira sighs at him, patting his hair back down as he tucks himself against her shoulder. "He's been in a mood today," she explains, and I shrug.

"That's just fine. He's a good boy." I wait for him to peek back out at me again, and I can't help but see my first son in his features. It's why I named him Weston, because Wesley was on my mind that day.

I swear, as I get older, I get more and more sentimental.

There's none of the old anger left for my first children and their betrayals. Some days, I wish they were still here. But... they tried to turn our children against me, almost ruined the family I had worked so hard to build. Luckily, Xoe never believed the hateful words they whispered when they thought I couldn't hear them.

Turning, I reach for her hand, squeezing it when she laces our fingers together, and I tug her toward the backdoor. "Let's show Richter the rest of the family."

He follows me obediently, and I can't help but smile to myself because he's doing so well right now—and he has no idea that I'm leading him directly away from where I'm sure Cleo and Sierra are camped out in their room once more.

As soon as we're outside, I can hear the kids laughing and it's one of my favorite sounds in the world. *Almost* as much as the sounds the older ones make when I take them to my room.

"Casey!" I call out, and he instantly stops chasing Owen to turn toward me. Even from this far away I can see that he's tense, his gaze sweeping over everyone outside before he heads our way through the snow. Of all my sons, Casey is the one I've raised the best. I have hope for Gavin and Owen and Weston, but they're still too young to know for sure. Casey though... he understands what it takes to keep a family together. He loves me and makes sure everyone else knows he loves them too.

"Daddy..." he says as he approaches, and I tilt my head to beckon him closer. Without hesitation, he steps forward and presses a kiss to my lips, his hand brushing my side before he stands back to look Richter over from head to toe.

Xoe tugs at his sleeve, and Casey's face turns from rigid and thoughtful into a bright smile.

"Sorry, Xoe," he says, leaning over to give her a kiss too, and she smiles back at him.

"Casey is my oldest boy," I explain, looking over at Richter to see him looking stiff, rigid. "He's probably about your age."

"I'm twenty-one," Richter declares proudly, as if he knows fuck-all at that age.

"Then you're a little bit older," I acknowledge, but I don't give him any more information as I turn back to Casey who has crossed his arms. He's defensive, standing between this outsider and the rest of our family, and I know he'd die to protect any one of them.

Fortunately, that's unnecessary.

"Richter is my brother, Casey. Family." The word carries weight in my house, and he slowly lets his hands drop. "Why don't you tell him who everyone is out here? I just showed him around inside."

"Yes, Daddy," Casey answers, shifting to the side so that Richter has a clear view of the wide space behind the house. He points off into the distance where the boys are tackling each other into the snow, laughing and shouting something at each other. "Over there is Owen—he's the younger one—and Gavin. That's my sister Brinnah behind them."

Richter stares out at them for a bit, watching Brinnah as she pelts Gavin with a snowball and then gets hit in return. He pulls his lower lip between his teeth, worrying it for a second before it pops free and he looks at me. "How many kids do you have, Bryden?"

"Right now? Thirteen," I answer, pride swelling in my chest again as I grin. "But we've got a couple more on the way."

"Hell..." he mutters under his breath, his gaze going unfocused as he lifts it back to the snowy mess in front of us.

There are crisscrossed tracks all over it, but with the snow-dusted trees in the background, it still looks beautiful—and nothing is more beautiful than seeing my family happy.

And that's what we are. Happy.

Happy and loved, each and every one of us.

Richter blows out a breath and then stands up straighter, trying to look like a man. He's not quite as tall as me or Casey, but it's possible he could gain another inch or so in the coming years if he hits a late growth spurt. That happened with Damon, but I'm still not sure just how tall he would have been if he hadn't lost his way.

Eventually, Richter's gaze swivels back to me and I know what he's going to say before the words even leave his lips.

"I want to see Cleo. Now."

TEN

Richter

Bryden smiles at me, but Casey glances at me with an even stare on his handsome face, careful to hide it from his father. It's obvious to me now that Bryden, even though he's older and less likely to harm any of these strong young kids, rules this household quite easily.

But unlike Dad, he does it with love.

Something I can't really remember feeling after Mom died. True, I've tried my best to love Skylar, and I do in a way, but she doesn't love me back and it's something I've come to live with. It doesn't make the days any easier, it just makes them bearable.

"Of course," Bryden says thoughtfully. "But I guess there are some rules I have to lay out before you do."

I turn to face him, nodding in agreement to terms that haven't even been discussed, then begin to walk away from Bryden and his son. There's more to this house that I haven't been privileged to see and I know that my sister has to be in one of the unexplored rooms.

"Richter."

The way Bryden says my name stops me in my tracks. I

close my eyes for a moment and take a shuddering breath because if I hadn't known any better, I could almost swear that Luke Greene himself had come to life to speak my name.

He's not Dad.

I tell that to myself over and over before I finally open my eyes again and glance at him over my shoulder. Xoe's standing on one side of him, Casey on the other, and while they look like the Gargoyles of Notre Dame protecting their own personal cathedral, he seems to be a lot more docile than his tone intended.

"The rules," he chides as he walks over and puts a hand on my shoulder.

I lower my eyes to his hand before I raise them again and stare into his, waiting.

"I already said yes," I say softly, shrugging out of his grip. "I just want to see my sister."

"*Our* sister," he corrects with a shake of his head. "We're all family here—or have you forgotten already?"

"You have my word that I'll do what you need me to if you just let me see Cleo," I repeat, taking a step away from him.

There's something about him that reminds me of Dad so much, and what worries me the most is that Bryden doesn't see it himself.

"Hm. Pinky promise?" he asks, holding up his hand. Against my better judgement and my need to see Cleo overpowering my good sense, I take his pinky in mine and shake.

We stop in the living room and Bryden sits in a leather recliner, motioning for me to sit in any of the available seats. Casey lingers near the entrance to a hallway, but I think it's due to an overwhelming need to protect his father.

From me? I wonder curiously. If I pose a threat to this family, then I've done something wrong already and I want to rectify that because if they see me as a threat, then my chances of seeing my sister are as good as gone.

"First, we need to correct the way you speak to me. I understand you want to see your sister, but I'm the man of this house and deserve to be treated with a modicum of respect," he begins thoughtfully as he rubs the bridge of his nose with a finger. "Once we get past that step, we can move on to the next one."

I blink rapidly a few times. He reminds me so much of my father in how he holds himself, and his mannerisms, that it makes me wonder if he sees me as a worthless child too.

But I'm not.

I'm a man now.

I have a house of my own. I'm trying to make a wife out of my sister, because that's what I was taught to do, and I'm trying to carry on the Greene name. I won't be able to keep my word to Dad if I don't have Cleo back in the house, though.

"Okay," I reply slowly. Clearing my throat, I run a hand back through my hair and shift in my seat. "I'm sorry if I snapped at you, I'm just really interested in seeing my sister and taking her off your hands. I'm sure you've done a wonderful job with her, but it's time she comes home where she belongs."

"She belongs with family, Richter," Bryden replies cheerfully.

"I know. That's what I said," I reply in confusion.

The man across the room from me turns his attention toward his son and nods at him. I watch carefully, waiting for Casey to enter and try to throw me out, but instead he turns around and walks out of the room.

Bryden lets out a heavy sigh as he stares at the now empty doorway. I can see something is weighing on his mind, but he seems to be enjoying his little game of mental cat and mouse and I can feel myself ready to shake answers out of him.

That's the Dad in me.

When something doesn't go my way, I lash out because it's what I'd seen done so many times.

Deep breath. Inhale, exhale; it'll all be okay.

And that's the Mom in me.

The level-headed coolness that falls over me, forcing me to calm the ire I feel building because I know it won't get me anywhere.

"I guess it's about time we had a talk, Richter. A real one. About family."

ELEVEN

Bryden

I rarely have to lecture my kids anymore. The older ones tend to do it for me because they know the rules of my house, they know my expectations—but Richter isn't mine.

He's blood, but... different. A brother is something completely new to me. Untested ground. I never got to know the only sibling I ever knew about. Jocelyn, who got me kicked out of Luke's house just because she was born, because she was the child he claimed so easily, but that's not Richter's fault.

Still, he needs to know the rules.

My rules.

So, I lecture and explain and encourage his questions. We talk about respect, about the need to love everyone in a family equally, and about the legacy of the Greene family.

Luke's legacy.

The legacy I know Richter is trying desperately to continue with his sister Skylar... and with Cleo.

He interrupts me several times to ask about her, but I remind him to be patient and eventually his questions turn to the *how* of my family. I tell him about my first children, Ella and Wesley, but I skim over the issues that put them in the ground. Instead, I focus on Xoe, mentioning Tristan and Damon only in passing before I bring him back to the wonderful, happy family still living under my roof. All of my children.

Thirteen beautiful lives—because I count Cleo among them—who have never spent a day wondering if they were loved, wanted, or welcome in this house.

That is the legacy *I* have created in the wake of Luke's decisions, and I can see the confusion and the hunger in Richter's eyes even though he won't speak it aloud. No, the more I've talked about how we all love each other, how we all contribute to the house and the raising of each new generation... the quieter Richter has become.

Brow furrowed, eyes dark like Luke's, but although he's blood... I can't tell exactly what he's thinking. All I can sense is the need to belong, and more than anything I want him to choose this family. To join us with his sister and bring the Greene legacy together.

No longer splintered and torn apart. Scattered by Luke's secrets.

But, *finally*, unified.

The sun has dipped below the horizon as I let my lecture wind down and allow Richter the silence to think—or at least as much silence as there ever is in my house. There's a buzz of activity in the kitchen where dinner is being prepared, the whirlwind of chaos from the younger ones that is a constant for me, but is likely distracting to him based on the way his eyes keep flicking to look at the family he didn't know he had. I understand it's overwhelming, and I wait patiently until Richter's gaze returns to mine.

"So they..." He gestures at everyone moving around the house, his voice tinged by something sad. "They all want this? They're all happy to come to your bed? To each other's?"

"Doesn't everyone want to be loved?" I ask in return, smiling at him as he seems to sag under the weight of whatever thoughts are driving him. It makes me want to reach out, to comfort him and so, gently, I add, "Don't *you* want to be loved, Richter?"

"I am loved," he snaps, sitting up straight again as his defensiveness returns. "Skylar loves me, and Cleo will too. We'll love each other."

I can hear the taint of doubt in his voice and I wonder if Richter didn't take after Luke in how he runs his house. Not out of love, but requirement. Obligation. The thought makes me worry for Skylar. Alone, with night coming on swiftly. But I know Richter won't leave to get her until he's seen Cleo, and I've made him wait long enough.

"I'm glad to know you and Skylar have been able to love each other. A family is not a family without love to hold it together." I smile and finally give in to the urge to reach over and squeeze his arm. "And I know Cleo will love you as well... in time."

"She's *my* sister, Bryden. She will love me."

I can't help but let my smile stretch as I tighten my grip on Richter's arm, feeling the tension buzzing in his muscles as he stiffens. "It's been a long time since you were together, Richter, and Cleo is sensitive. She doesn't like change, and although you remember her very well... she was only five when she joined my family. I'm just asking you to be patient with her, and to not upset her."

"I know how my sister is and I want to see her. Please,"

Richter adds the last word through almost gritted teeth, but I release his arm in recognition of the respect he's offered.

"Of course. We're about to have dinner anyway," I acknowledge, looking toward the doorway where Casey has reappeared, lingering throughout our talk. Raising my voice, I call out, "Cleo! Come to the living room."

It takes a minute, but then I hear the giggles as Cleo and Sierra leave their makeshift fort. Cleo appears in the doorway in an oversized sweatshirt, a big smile on her face as she walks over to me. "Yes, Daddy?"

"There's someone here who would like to talk to you," I answer, accepting her kiss before she slips onto my lap.

"Cleo! I've been looking for you for so long." Richter leans forward, reaching for her with so much urgency in his voice, but Cleo jerks back, hiding her face against my shoulder as I raise a hand to stop him.

"Patience, remember? You can't force love," I admonish, brushing my hand up and down Cleo's back. She makes a soft sound, peeking at Richter with wary eyes as she fists the fabric of my shirt. "Cleo, sweetheart, this is Richter. Your brother."

"Richter?" she repeats, and I can see there's a flicker of recognition in her sweet face, but she doesn't reach for him. Not yet, and I don't think she would without my permission anyway.

"Yes, Cleo, it's me. Richter. Your brother. You remember me, right?" he asks, the desperation for acceptance so clear in his wide eyes.

"He's part of our family," I explain, keeping to the simple concepts that guide my house as I bring my other hand to her belly. Feeling the firmness of it through the sweatshirt as she lays her hand over mine.

"He's family," she repeats, and I look back at Richter to see fire in his gaze as his eyes bounce from my face, to Cleo's, to her stomach, and back again.

"That's right," I confirm, smiling. "And we love everyone in our family equally."

TWELVE

Richter
___

Bryden tells me to be patient with Cleo, and even though I know what's best for her, I find it hard to contain the excitement in seeing her again. She's the perfect image of Mom and Dad but still special in her own way.

She's the brightest star in the Heavens when there should be none, and it breaks my heart that she doesn't seem to really remember me when I always looked out for her as best as I could.

Of course, time does that to anyone with a mind that's *right*, and hers is *left*—in a constant struggle of trying to find a normalcy even though she doesn't realize it herself.

Bryden is watching us with a warm smile on his face, content in the fact that another family bond is forming in his proverbial house of love, but she doesn't belong here and neither do I.

I'll sit through his bullshit family dinner. I'll act like everything makes perfect sense and his way is the only way since I'm under his roof. But he's not a Greene—he never will be, and I know how families should really be run because Dad showed me.

When we get to the table, I pull out the chair next to me and smile hopefully at Cleo, but she goes to sit next to that Sierra girl without so much as a second glance in my direction. I feel completely defeated when I haven't even been given the chance to really try yet.

Once his entire family is seated, he takes his place at the head of the table. It reminds me of one of the last days I spent with Mom. She had Cleo next to her, helping her eat her supper with Dad watching, disdain in his eyes. Maybe he never really loved Cleo, or if he did, he had a funny fucking way of showing it.

I think he wanted all of his children to be perfect, and because she wasn't, he didn't waste time getting to really know her. There was only once that I can remember him giving two shits about being with her and that's when he left with her and she didn't come back.

He admonished Mom for busting up his truck over it. Hand and fist. Words and darkness. That's how Dad ruled his home and it worked for him.

Sometimes, I can feel myself slipping into his mindset, but I remind myself that I have a choice. I can choose to be like him, or I can choose to be like Mom.

They war with each other inside of me. Both sides of a coin that should have never been flipped—a constant reminder that no matter how good I try to be, there's always that part of Luke inside of me lurking, ready to strike.

"Help yourself."

I glance to my left and nod at Casey who's holding out a large, white, ceramic bowl toward me. I use the ladle to dump a portion of mashed potatoes on my plate, then pass the bowl to my right.

I'm not hungry.

My stomach is sour right now over the thought of

eating, no matter how good it smells, because my sister doesn't seem to care that I'm here.

They eat in silence, with the occasional giggle coming from Cleo and Sierra. I steal a glance at Bryden who's enjoying his meal, completely undisturbed by the fact that the two of them are having a little jousting match with their forks between bites.

No one seems to notice, and if they do, they don't care. It's so much different than being at a table with Dad.

When we ate in silence, it's because it was commanded. He always told us ahead of time when he didn't feel like listening to his 'useless fucking kids' bickering at the dinner table, and we obliged him.

We ate in fear, whereas everyone here seems to be content, happy, and carefree.

The way Mom would have wanted it, I think glumly as I place an elbow on the table and rest my cheek against the palm of my hand.

I let out a heavy sigh.

I don't want to be disrespectful to Bryden or his home, but I want Cleo to remember who I am, so I do the one thing I think might spark a solid memory of me.

I reach over for the bread on my plate, rip off a small piece, then toss it across the table.

She looks up at me when it smacks her forehead and I smile. It's a game the three of us would play when Dad walked away from the dinner table—something that Mom would allow because she knew it was the only fun we could really have sitting in our chairs without talking.

She furrows her brow for a moment, then swats the piece of bread away from where it landed on her lap, and then she goes back to fork-jousting with Sierra.

I clear my throat as I rip off a bigger piece, then roll it

between the palms of my hands, before I steal another glance at Bryden who's watching me with amusement.

I blanch, but he shakes his head kindly, then nods. I turn my eyes back toward Cleo since I have the approval of her 'father' and toss a bread ball at her again.

This time she looks angry until I hook my fingers into my mouth and stick my tongue out at her.

I can almost see it starting to sink in. The memory of her brother, who was much younger than he is now, doing his best to make his sisters happy and keep their Mom safe.

She looks away for a moment.

Come on, remember, I will her in desperate silence.

And when her face suddenly crumples and she begins to cry, I think she finally does.

THIRTEEN

Bryden

The boy upset Cleo—the one fucking thing I told him not to do. I can feel the anger buzzing like a hornet's nest in my chest, a promise of violence if I don't rein in my control.

Stay calm.

Forcing a slow breath, I push back from the table and stand, keeping my hands flat on the wood on either side of my plate. The boy turns to look at me, and I shake my head slowly. *"Tsk, tsk,* Richter. I believe I asked you to be patient, to not upset our dear Cleo."

"I was just helping—"

"I think it's time for you to go home." I cut him off, keeping my voice steady. "I'm sure your sister is waiting for you, and I know you wouldn't want her to be alone tonight." I'm offering him a graceful exit, which is more than he deserves for the disrespect he's shown. Glancing out the back windows at the last weak rays of the sun, I continue, "Let's get you on your way before the light leaves us."

"But I— NO!" Richter shouts, standing up so fast his chair rocks back and it's only Heather's quick reflexes that keep it from tumbling. A few of my children gasp, but no one speaks.

"It's time for you to leave, Richter." It's easy to keep my voice level, but the only person in the house that doesn't seem to recognize the pending threat in the air is the boy glaring at me across the table.

"Like hell I'm leaving without her!" Richter's chest is pumping, harsh breaths moving in and out as he finally tears his eyes from me in the eerie silence that has settled over the room. He reaches across the table for Cleo, but my girl keeps rubbing her face, sniffling softly. "Cleo, you need to come home with me. Come home to me and Skylar."

He wants her to betray me, to betray her family.
Not a chance.

The strap is still hanging on the nail in the hall and I honestly can't remember the last time I had to use it—but that doesn't mean I won't. Brother or not, he's still young and clearly in need of discipline. Cleo doesn't look at him, and a smile spreads over my lips as I watch his desperation overflow, his need for love so clear and sad that I almost pity him, and it helps to calm my anger.

"Cleo will not be going anywhere tonight, Richter. You and Skylar are welcome to come back tomorrow to talk with her, but you are leaving. Alone. *Now*." I can feel the tension humming through me, a chuckle rumbling through my chest as he turns to stare at me defiantly. "Trust me, you do *not* want to argue with me, boy."

"I'm not a boy!" he snaps, and I let the laugh roll out.

"All right, brother, then show me. Leave my home respectfully, like a man, so I can welcome you and Skylar back tomorrow."

Richter hesitates and I can see the emotions flitting across his face in waves. Anger and hurt and defiance and sadness. He thought he was coming to rescue his sister, to bring her home, but after everything I've shown him today, he seems to have missed the most important point—Cleo is already home. Cleo already has a family, and if he wants to be a part of that family... he's going to have to follow the rules.

My rules.

"Richter." I say his name and it seems to break his trance as a muscle in his jaw twitches.

"I'll be back tomorrow, Cleo. With Skylar. Then we'll all go home together." Those last few words are spoken with his eyes focused on mine. A promise, possibly a threat, but I'm not worried. Richter learned everything at Luke's feet, just as I did, but he never got sent away, which means he likely missed out on the most important lesson of all. Loving everyone, equally, so that no one feels abandoned or left out.

Like he'd left Skylar alone today.

Letting my smile stretch, I ignore his aggression and tilt my head toward the door. "Let me walk you out."

I turn on my heel and lead the way. He hesitates, but a moment later I hear his shoes on the wood, the creak of the floorboards as he follows in my wake.

"I'm coming back tomorrow," he says under his breath, giving me a serious look that reveals the Luke in his eyes.

"Wonderful. I look forward to meeting Skylar, and I'm sure Cleo will enjoy another visit."

Whatever Richter wants to say in response, he bites it back, his jaw tightening before he nods stiffly. I open the door with a smile, and he grabs his coat, marching outside toward his truck without another comment.

Probably the smartest thing he could have done under the circumstances, because I'm not sure what I might have done if he'd spoken to me disrespectfully again in front of my family.

There are lines that shouldn't be crossed. Lines that Richter doesn't seem to know about, and that means I'll have to be patient with him—just like I asked him to be patient with Cleo.

It's only fair, after all, but that doesn't mean I won't correct him if he steps too far.

Keeping my family together is all that matters, and it will be up to Richter if he wants to be a part of that family or not.

"Is everything okay, Daddy?" Casey steps up beside me, glancing out the front door where we can both see Richter turning his truck around to leave.

"Of course." I reach over and squeeze his shoulder, smiling at my eldest living boy. "He's young, son. And I think he's been alone a long time, both he and Skylar. They just need to get to know us, to see what their life could be like."

"I don't like how he speaks to you." Casey turns to look at me, and I can see the strength in him. The strength he'll need to keep this family together, to keep it going—and I'm not sure if I saw that same strength in Richter.

"I know, son." Leaning forward, I press a quick kiss to his lips and repeat what I'm telling myself. "We need to be patient with him. And Skylar."

"Yes, Daddy," he answers, dipping his head before he walks back to the table. I give one more glance out the front door to confirm that Richter has gone home to his sister before I shut the front door and return to the kitchen.

My family is all sitting quietly, hands off the table, waiting for me. Even Cleo has stopped crying, her reddened nose and cheeks a beautiful display as she looks toward me.

Everyone knows their place in this house. Everyone is respectful and so well-behaved. Only the little ones are squirming, and that's because they're tired.

"Thank you for waiting," I say, taking my seat back at the head of the table. "Hopefully we'll see Richter and Skylar tomorrow, but for now let's finish dinner."

"Yes, Daddy," everyone choruses in response, and as I pick up my fork, everyone returns to eating, but with less joy than before. Richter disturbed the peace of my house. He brought sad news, disrupted our lives… but he brought something else too.

Hope.

The possibility of bringing the Greene family together. Making us whole. For that, I'll let his disrespect go tonight. I modeled the patience I expect from him, and now he has no excuse if he misbehaves again.

And, if there is a next time, he'll see that I'm my father's son. Luke's first born. His heir. Then Richter will learn exactly what happens to those who don't follow the rules.

FOURTEEN

Skylar

―――――

This is what true loneliness feels like, I think as I wrap my arms around myself. I'm sitting on the same stoop that Mom did when Dad left with Cleo. I have the same empty feeling in my heart because I know that if Richter comes home, it won't be with our sister.

These Greene men are all the same.

Headstrong and only keeping what serves them the best, but I would hope that the Mom in him would at least convince him to honestly give a damn about Cleo if not me.

I run my hands back through my hair, then clasp them together on the back of my neck. My legs are shaking as I do my best to sit here and believe that my brother hasn't abandoned me.

Life isn't all that great right now, but I know it would be worse without him.

How did Darby do all of this without breaking?

I miss her.

Especially in this newfound loneliness that's gripping my heart. My mother may not have been the strongest woman in the world physically, but she bore more on her back and in her soul than Dad would have ever been capable of.

With a sigh, I lift my face and glance toward the driveway, tears springing to my eyes when I see no sign of light on the horizon. Of course, I should be used to that by now. The only time we'd ever seen light in this fucking house would be when Mom would help us with our studies, cuddle us after Dad laid into us, and kissed our cuts and scrapes when we fell.

Get back up. No matter how many times you fall, you get right back on your feet. It will always make you stronger.

A tear rolls down my cheek as I think of what Mom always told us. I don't know much about our grandmother really, but I doubt she got up as many times as Mom did. We'd hide in the shadows when she and Dad would argue. We'd see him hit her and watch her get right back up and in his face. We saw when she hit him first and his reaction confused us. Almost as though he approved of the action, and I think that's where Richter gets that from—the confusion, not the lesson.

I don't really believe there was anything in this house that we could have learned from Dad, only from Mom.

I get to my feet and brush the dirt off the back of my jeans. I don't know if I ever really loved my father, but I did love my mother and I'll do my best to make her proud.

One last glance up the driveway and I shake my head as I turn on my heel and push the front door open, locking it again so he doesn't know I was outside.

I'll have to hide the key before he gets home, *if* he does.

Maybe Richter will come home, maybe he won't. However, if he's got any *real* Greene blood in him, he'll be the good man that Mom always wanted him to be and leave Cleo where she is.

She deserves better than this.
We all do.

I startle when the front door opens and closes about twenty minutes later. I had almost fallen asleep on the couch watching some old reruns, but now I'm wide awake again.

Hoping that my sister is somewhere far away from the desperation and depravity that hangs low in the air of this home, staining the walls and beds alike.

"Skylar!"

I sit up and rub my eyes.

Richter sounds frantic, angry, and a little worried.

He probably thinks I ran away.

I chuckle despite the mood I've been in for most of my life after Mom. He always seems to forget that I've already tried that once, and when he caught me, into the oubliette I went for a solid seven days.

I think being in there under his rage has to be worse than Dad's because at least he would allow for small meals to be tossed in sometimes and bottles of water on occasion.

Richter's anger dictates scraps from the table and piss sprayed down into the darkness.

And even through all of it, he swears that he loves me and that we'll be happiest in this home as husband and wife —a request I have yet to acquiesce to.

"Are you okay?" I ask him after I find him pacing the kitchen floor. Richter looks a little disheveled, which isn't something I'm used to.

"I found her," he says, glancing over at me as he continues walking back and forth. "I found Cleo."

I bite back a sigh of relief. It seems that he had the good common sense to leave her where she was after all.

"How is she doing?" I ask curiously as I cross my arms loosely over my chest.

Richter stops pacing almost instantly and rubs a hand irritably over his face. He's getting angry and if his temper explodes, I'll be on the receiving end of his mood. I have to be careful now considering I've sassed him enough in the past few days and have the sore lip to prove it.

His shoulders slump slightly as the air of anger leaves his body in a *whoosh*. "Honestly? I think she's doing great without me."

His tone is so full of dejection that I walk over and wrap my arms around him. As nothing more than his little sister who loves him dearly and wants him to know that nothing that's happened to Cleo—good or bad—after Dad sent her off to God knows where, is in any way his fault.

When Richter shifts in my embrace and lowers his face toward mine, I let him go and take a step back. I know it will only add to his frustration, but I can't reconcile anything about this being right.

He sucks his teeth for a moment before he walks past me and I follow him because that's what good Greene women do.

"Sit down," he tells me in a stern tone after he takes a seat in Dad's favorite recliner. He clears his throat as he leans forward and rests his elbows against his knees.

I do my best not to laugh out loud, because it's almost like staring at the man himself when my brother is like this.

"Cleo's fine," he begins curtly as he rubs his face irritably again. "And that's what bothers me. She lives with some weird family, in this commune environment, and you know what the kicker is? The guy that runs the place says he's our brother. More Greenes have been out in the fucking world and we never knew about it," he finishes bitterly.

The taste in my mouth becomes sour and the thumping of my heart quickens. Another Greene male is not something this world needs. Hell, if I'm being honest with myself, Richter is already one too many.

This entire fucking debacle should have died with Dad.

"She doesn't remember me. At least, I don't think so," he continues as he blows out his breath and leans back in the chair. I watch as he folds an arm behind his head and glances out the window, feeling like I'm looking at a ghost that I would rather forget. But I guess when the blood of Luke Greene burns like lava inside your veins, it's inevitable to see him from time to time.

"Remember when we used to sit at the table with Mom and Dad? Remember how I used to throw bread at her?" he asks, pursing his lips for a moment. I nod even though I know he's not looking at me because he'll just assume that I've agreed with him anyway. "I tried that, you know? I figured if anything would help Cleo figure out who I was, it would be that. And you know what she did, Skylar? She cried."

I sit in silence for a moment trying to choose my next words carefully because he's a little volatile right now and it's scaring me.

"She probably has bad memories about this place, Richter. You remember how Dad treated her, don't you? You were the one that kept us safe from him when you could, and Mom too. You were the man of this house when you shouldn't have been burdened with it, and Cleo is probably afraid that Dad is still here."

"Bryden, that's the guy who runs the place, says that I

can go back tomorrow but he wants you to come too. He wants us both to be there the next time I go see Cleo, and this time, I'm not coming back without her. You'll help me, won't you?"

I turn my eyes toward the ceiling in frustration. He's completely bypassed everything I said to him because he so desperately wants to be right.

"Skylar?" he presses, his tone becoming stern.

I close my eyes for a moment before I open them again and look at my brother across the room from me. 'No' is not something these men understand either, but what I do will be for Cleo and not him.

One of us has to have some kind of chance in this world, no matter how muddled her brain may be.

I lick my lips nervously and nod.

I'll go back with him, I'll ask Bryden if I can speak to him alone, and I'll tell him everything that Richter has done to me in a bid to keep Cleo far away from these walls.

"Good," he says in relief as he gets to his feet. He comes over to me and extends a hand down. "I'm going to need some help falling asleep."

I grit my teeth but take his hand and let him lead me upstairs to our bedroom. Nothing good ever came from telling a Greene man 'no' because they don't understand it regardless.

As he pushes the door to our room open, I reach up and pull my hair back into a tight ponytail, walk over to the dresser, and retrieve a hairband to hold it in place.

Richter's already sitting on the edge of the bed, leaning back on the palms of his hands. With a deep breath, I drop down to my knees and unzip his jeans.

I pull his dick through the fly of his underwear, wrapping my hand around it while I try to send my mind somewhere else. As I take the head of it into my mouth and begin to move skillfully up and down his length, I tell myself that tomorrow will be different because whoever this Bryden person is, he'll see that this is all wrong, and he'll help me set Richter straight.

FIFTEEN

Bryden

It takes a bit longer than usual for the little ones to get to sleep, and I know that's because of the chaos of the day. Yet, now that the house is winding down, I can feel peace returning, and while I listen to my older children brushing their teeth and getting ready for bed, I can't help but smile as I step out onto the back porch, breathing in the frigid air.

I'm really a lucky man.

They're all good kids, and that's because I've become a better father over the years. More consistent. The younger ones know what's expected of them as they grow up, how the way we love each other grows as they do.

Ella and Wesley just... didn't have anyone setting a good example for them.

My gaze drifts over to the tree line where I know they are. Beside their mother, Marian, who tried to abandon us. Underneath the tree where Ella tried to hang herself when she was carrying Tristan. The rush of rage that memory summons still feels fresh, raw, and I can remember the way Wesley screamed like it was yesterday. If the branch hadn't snapped, I don't know where I'd be now. I don't know where any of us would be. Each of my beautiful children wouldn't exist if she'd succeeded... but I never gave her the chance to betray us like that again.

It hurt me to lock her in the closet those days after, especially after Wesley admitted *why* she'd done it as she screamed and cried through the door.

She was pregnant with our first child, and whether it was mine or Wesley's didn't matter to me—it was still mine. As much as Ella and Wesley were mine. And she'd tried to take it from me, tried to abandon us just like her Mama did.

I'd bought the stuff to make her chain that week because I couldn't trust her not to try and hurt herself or the baby. Wesley had begged me not to chain her up, but he'd failed to protect his sister and his weakness only upset me more. Just like with Marian, I had to be the strong one. I had to make the tough decisions to keep our family together. So, Ella stayed in my room unless I escorted her to the table to eat. Ankle chained to the bed so she couldn't do anything that stupid again, given just enough slack to reach the bathroom if she needed it.

My cock twitches as I remember her belly swollen and round. Each time she looked beautiful. Tristan first, then my beautiful Xoe, and then Damon. I'm still convinced that Damon was Wesley's offspring, he had his weakness, his subtle defiant streak. That's why he had to go in the ground as he grew older. I didn't need him questioning me in front of the little ones or trying to run with them like Tristan had.

That bitch.

Just thinking of Tristan has my teeth grinding. She gave me Casey, and Sierra, but that's the only good thing she did with her pathetic life. The girl was never obedient, never grateful for the love I shared with her. She tried so hard to turn my Xoe against me, and after Sierra was born I knew she had to go. I put her in the ground right next to Ella, my first born who had whispered poison in our daughter's ear from birth.

In the dark I know I can't really see the place where their bodies lay, but I know it by heart. I dug each grave by hand, just like I had for Stephanie. Sometimes my hands bled, staining the handle of the shovel, but that was my punishment for allowing weakness, disobedience. For tolerating their betrayals.

And it was all worth it.

I haven't had to put anyone in the ground since Damon. Xoe was heartbroken, but she understood that he couldn't be allowed to taint the children. We couldn't lose another generation to their quiet defiance—and we didn't. Together, Xoe and I raised a family that understood what it meant to be loved. *Really* loved, with no exceptions, no favoritism.

Letting out a slow breath, I watch it turn into fog on the breeze and I feel at peace with my choices. Death is never pretty, but it is sometimes necessary to protect what matters most—and family matters more than anything to me.

"Daddy," Casey says as he leans out the door, trying not to intrude on my thoughts, but I smile at him.

"Come join me, son." The chill is sinking through my long-sleeved shirt, and I know I should have grabbed my coat, but I really just wanted to stand out here for a few minutes. As Casey steps up beside me, I glance over at him, at the strong profile cast in shadow by the dim light coming through the windows. He's handsome, and I know his sisters enjoy his bed as much as mine, and he always loves them equally like a good brother should. I smile a little as I turn my eyes back to the forest spread out behind the house. "How is Sierra doing?"

Casey shrugs, scuffing his shoe on the concrete as he

chooses his words carefully. "She's okay, Daddy, but... you know what she wants."

"I do," I reply with a nod, watching another cloud of breath float away from me on the breeze. "Still no success?"

"Not yet." He shrugs, shoving his hands into the pockets of his jeans to keep them warm. "She had her woman time last week, and she was upset, but she wants to keep trying."

"That's my girl," I say with a smile, but I can feel the sadness lingering in my chest. She's seventeen, the same age as Heather, but her sister has already brought two children into the family... and Sierra hasn't managed to get pregnant even once. I know it bothers her, that it hurts to see her sisters swell with life, and I know just how often Casey loves her as he does his best to help.

"Daddy... she wants me to love her again tonight, but I know—"

"It's okay, Casey. Show your sister you love her, and maybe this time she'll be as fortunate as her sisters." I reach over and squeeze his shoulder. "You're a good brother to her."

"Thank you, Daddy," he replies, smiling at me in that lopsided way that reminds me of Wesley for a flash before it disappears. "So, what should I tell Moira?"

"You were going to love Moira tonight?" I ask, keeping my voice light, and he nods. "Well, then I'll just have her in my bed tonight. Xoe and Heather know that they have to share my love."

"Yes, Daddy," Casey answers, glancing back inside through the windows, and I watch his eyes narrow as he looks over the cribs where the little ones are sleeping. I know we need to go in, that I need to check the kitchen so everyone can go to bed, but I hesitate.

"Casey, I know it's been a while since I brought you to

my bedroom, but I want you to know that I love you very much, son."

"I love you too, Daddy, and I know how important it is to keep the girls happy." He looks down, scuffing his shoe on the concrete again. "Maybe after Sierra is pregnant?"

"I wouldn't make you wait that long, son. We'll talk about it tomorrow." Reaching over, I grab him gently by the neck and pull him close. His lips meet mine with no hesitation, and I squeeze the tense muscles at the base of his skull as I show him how loved he is. How much I appreciate him helping me to carry our line forward.

As I break the kiss, I keep hold of him for a moment longer. Studying his expression, the honest love he has for me, and I wonder if Richter will ever look at me like this.

My instincts say no, but that's okay. We can make it work, and I know we need more males of-age in the house. Casey knows it too, even if he's as unsure of Richter as I am.

"It won't be like this forever, son," I say. "Gavin and Owen will be old enough soon."

"I know, Daddy." He gives me another lopsided smile and I release him, turning to open the door into the house.

The kitchen is perfect, and I really only check it now for consistency. Routines help everyone to understand their place, their responsibilities, which means mistakes happen less often.

"Good job, everyone. I hope you sleep well," I say, dismissing them with a smile before I add, "Moira, stay and talk to me."

I catch the flicker of disappointment on Xoe and Heather's faces, but they don't say anything as they head to bed. Casey pulls Sierra to the side before the hall, and I'm soothed by the bright smile on her face. It's not her fault that she can't get pregnant, but after all this time I'm pretty confident there's something wrong inside her. Casey and I have both shown her our love again and again... but it just hasn't worked.

Someday we'll have to have that conversation, but not now. She's sensitive, similar to Cleo, and I'll let her hold out hope for a while longer.

"Is everything okay, Daddy?" Moira asks, pulling my attention back to her. One of her dimples appears on her cheek as she smiles at me, and I return it so she knows she's not in trouble.

"Yes, darling. I just wanted you to join me in my room tonight." Reaching for her hand, I squeeze it firmly. "Don't worry about your brother though, I asked Casey to share his bed with Sierra instead."

"Thank you, Daddy," she answers, and I love the way she squeezes my hand back, already taking a step toward my room like a good girl.

"I'm sorry it's been so long since you've shared my bed," I add as I take the lead.

"It's okay, Daddy." Moira shrugs a little as we turn down the hall and go into my room. I close the door and lean against the wall to watch her undress. Socks, pants, shirt, underwear, all folded beside the door.

"You haven't felt unloved, have you?" I ask, reaching over to trace my fingers over the round of her breast. They're swollen since she's still nursing Weston, and it's something I love to watch.

"No, Daddy!" She reaches up to touch my arm, sincerity burning in her blue eyes. "Never! I know that you love us all equally, and I know that Heather needs to feel your love more often than me. She gets... unsure sometimes, and I never want her to feel that way."

Really?

"Heather spends a lot of time in my bed," I answer, putting a chastising edge to my tone. "She knows that she can't expect to be with me every day, just like Xoe can't."

"She knows, Daddy. She just gets sad sometimes, and you always make her happy again."

"Do I make you happy, Moira?" I ask, pulling her over to the bed, and I love the pink that rises into her cheeks.

"Yes, Daddy."

"Good," I reply, feeling my grin spread as I nudge her onto the sheets and she lays down on her back, knees apart. "You're such a good girl, Moira, I'd never want you to feel left out, or unloved, or unhappy."

"I don't, Daddy. I promise." Her chest starts to rise and fall faster as I slide my hands over her thighs, pushing them farther apart.

"That makes *me* very happy to hear," I say, just before I lean forward to trace my tongue through her folds. Each of my girls tastes a little different, but they all remind me of Ella. So pure and all mine.

When she starts to make those soft sounds, I focus on her clit, flicking it with my tongue until my quiet girl finally starts to be more vocal. Moving two fingers inside gets a moan, and I concentrate on making her come. She deserves to feel good, she's earned this attention from me, and I can only hope that I've taught Casey well enough to provide this for the girls. And since Gavin and Owen share a room with him, I hope he's passing it along. Teaching them their responsibilities to their family while he shares his love with Sierra.

"Daddy!" Moira cries out, and I feel her pussy grasping at my fingers as her wetness surges. I'm grinning when I stand up, licking my fingers clean of her taste, because that *might* have been loud enough to be heard through the walls.

"You're being a very good girl tonight, Moira," I praise, watching her pant and squirm on the bed as I remove my clothes.

"Thank you, Daddy," she replies breathily, and I love the way she reaches between her thighs to touch herself. Making sure she's ready for me. Moira deserves more of my attention, more of my time... after all, she's the only one of my living daughters besides Xoe to have given me a son, and our family will need more sons if we want to grow.

There will come a day when I won't be able to share my love, when it will be my time to go in the ground, and I want the Greene family to be prepared to continue on.

Putting another son in Moira is a good way to help that along.

"I should be thanking *you*, sweetheart," I say as I climb onto the bed. "That was beautiful, and I'm going to show you just how thankful I am."

SIXTEEN

Richter

I wake up the next morning feeling indifferent. I had a lot of anger, and even more sadness swelling inside me when I left Bryden's home.

Anger that he treated me like a child, even though I probably deserved it. Sadness that Cleo didn't recognize me right away... and because of the stark difference in how he's raised his children as opposed to Dad's way.

Skylar shifts slightly on the bed next to me and I turn my face toward her. She looks so much like Mom that in some ways I feel like I'm doing the right thing. Darby was a beautiful woman—strong, full of life, and defiant at every turn.

She gave Dad hell and I know that the three of us secretly enjoyed it. I refuse to believe that Cleo didn't have fun when Mom would give Dad's shit right back to him, because I would see her hiding her smile behind her little hands.

A sigh escapes me as I run my hands over my face briefly. The indifference is turning into sadness again, and I know that when I get back to Bryden's house I'll need to have a good, clear head on my shoulders.

Turning on my side as gently as I can, I lick the tips of my fingers then slip them into my would-be wife's panties. She stirs slightly but doesn't push me away, which tells me that she's still asleep.

I'm gentle with her as I begin to circle her clit with my forefinger. And when she stirs again, I smile.

Skylar may never admit that she likes when I touch her, but I know she does. She has free will and she can tell me no any time she chooses, but she's afraid that I'll do to her what Dad did to Mom, so she placates me as best as she can while keeping her head above ground.

In every sense of the word.

As I slip a finger into her damp opening, I purse my lips and lean my head against my pillow. My eyes move from her face to the wall behind her.

Another sigh.

Another feeling of sadness threatening to overwhelm me.

I close my eyes briefly as I move another finger into her pussy and place my thumb on her clit.

Little moments like this help me see things clearly, and as I begin to slowly move my fingers in and out of her core, I can't help but wonder how Cleo's would feel.

By right, I should have two wives, though I doubt she would understand what was being done to her.

Even though...

I grit my teeth at the thought. Bryden put his hand on Cleo's stomach—an obvious gesture to let me know that what was mine to claim has already been taken.

But he can't take this from me, I think as I slip my fingers out of Skylar and wipe them clean on my shorts. I move closer to her, reach for the waistband of her panties, and pull the delicate material off her body.

I toss them over the side of the bed and scoot down between her legs, wrapping my hands around her thighs before leaning in to inhale her sweet scent.

Next to Mom's, it's my favorite thing in the world.

And I only ever smelled Mom when she would console us after Dad laid into us, or when she found time to play with us as a distraction to what she had been suffering in abject silence.

"Richter?" Skylar's voice is groggy as she shifts on the bed. She's not completely aware that I want her to perform her wifely duties right now, but she will be shortly.

I glance up at her for a moment and smile as she uses the palms of her hands to rub her eyes. If I want her to be compliant, I have to move quickly.

Lowering my face between her legs again, I flick my tongue against her clit, which elicits a sharp gasp from her.

I've always been fond of waking her up like this, and I hope that maybe one day she'll wake me up in a similar fashion.

As soon as her body goes rigid, I slip my tongue into her. She'll never tell me no, and I think it's because she loves me more than she's willing to admit, though I wish she would at the very least be a much more active participant in our loving moments.

I push my tongue as far into her as it will go before I begin moving it in and out. It's something that I know she likes—which she's too stubborn to admit. I may be the man of this house but, unlike Dad, I believe this should be a pleasurable thing for the both of us.

Skylar's body begins to tremble as I move my tongue from her pussy to her clit. There's no way she's close already, and if she fakes another one, I'm going to lose my shit.

She knows better.

Love takes time and is a beautiful thing—it has to be cherished, not rushed.

Even so, I can feel my dick pressing against my shorts, begging for release, and I decide that maybe this time I'll let her get off easy.

I let go of her legs, push myself up to my knees, and pull my shorts off. Skylar, being her usual self, turns her face away and reaches her hands behind her head to grip the bedsheets. She doesn't like to hold me or touch me when we're loving each other, but that has to change if we're ever going to be parents.

She'll have to learn to hold our children—to love them when the time comes, and she'll be a better woman for it.

I grab my dick and press it against her opening, causing her to whimper slightly.

"Don't cry," I half-beg, half-command her. "This is how we're supposed to love each other."

Before the protest that I know is coming has a chance to leave her lips, I push myself inside her.

Skylar gasps as I grit my teeth.

She's still so tight after all of the attempts we've made so far to become parents and Dad told me that means that she isn't cheating on me. He said that if I ever loved her and felt her walls looser than normal, that some other man was sticking his dick into my property.

But Skylar's a good girl, and as I lean down to kiss her, my hips moving slowly, I know that she'd never cheat on me.

Good girls don't leave their husbands.

They give them a family to love, to teach, and to guide.

And that's exactly what Skylar is going to give me.

I use my hand to wipe away the fog on the bathroom mirror. I had Skylar shower with me so that I could clean her up. While I do love the smell of me on her, I love her scent alone better.

I glance at her in the mirror, watching as she uses the towel to dry herself off, but she gets dressed as quickly as she can, and I chuckle.

Turning my eyes back to my own reflection, I wait until she leaves the room before I remove the towel from around my waist and run it against my body, making sure that I smell like the body wash and nothing more.

I crack my neck as I toss the towel into the hamper, then pull open the medicine cabinet.

In a weird way, Bryden and his family presented rather nicely, which took me by surprise considering how many of them there are. Today, I want to extend that same courtesy, so I reach for Dad's bottle of aftershave and apply a generous amount to my face and neck.

If what Bryden says about Dad is true, then he should know the scent when it hits him. If he doesn't, then he's a fucking liar like the little voice in my head has been whispering to me, and I'll take Cleo by force if I have to.

Deep down inside, no matter how much I try to fight it, I know I'm more Luke than Darby and I'll have to tip the scales to bring my family back together again.

Dad may have torn us apart in a bid to get back at Mom, but I'm going to reclaim what's mine.

And as I begin to get dressed, I know that's what Mom would have wanted.

Even if she wouldn't have wanted it like this.

SEVENTEEN

Bryden

I've been watching the clock all morning as my family has worked through our usual routines. Breakfast, chores, and now everyone is settling into schoolwork.

Either teaching, or learning.

I think my family does a much better job than traditional schools ever could. Stephanie was able to teach me how to read in less than a year, and she was always looking for new and interesting things for me to learn. Luke didn't always support it, but Stephanie made sure I understood how important it was to be educated. And even though that stopped when she was put in the ground, when I got kicked out and had to go to public school, the teachers said I did very well for someone who was homeschooled.

Not a straight-A student, but I passed with a mix of grades. Math was always my weakness, but I have a grasp on the important things, and I've made sure each of my children is educated. They know how to read, how to add and subtract, multiply and divide—and more importantly they know how to survive.

The garden we've built in the backyard will return in

the Spring and provide us with vegetables and a few treats like watermelon. We've even learned how to can the produce so we don't waste a single bit of what we grow. Keeping my family strong and healthy year-round.

I wonder if Richter and Skylar have had the same benefits.

Did Luke teach them? Did their mother?

Was their mother Jocelyn?

"Everything okay, Daddy?" Xoe asks, and I feel her hands slide over my shoulders, her thumbs digging in to ease the tension I didn't even realize I was holding.

"I'm wonderful. Even better now," I add with a smile as I look up at her behind my chair.

"I'm glad." Xoe smiles down at me while she continues the massage, working at the knots in my shoulders as I zone out on the kids studying on the floor. "Daddy?"

"Yes, Xoe?"

"Is... Richter coming back today?" Her voice is quiet, hushed, as if she doesn't want the others in the room to hear it.

"I hope so," I reply honestly, glancing at the clock on the mantle of the fireplace again. It's almost eleven, and that means preparations for lunch will begin soon.

Do we prepare an extra plate? Two?

Clearing my throat, I reach up and tug at Xoe's wrist, pulling her around the chair and into my lap. She's wearing a dress, even as cold as it is outside, and I know it's because she's hoping I'll touch her... and, honestly, I could use the distraction.

"Did you get the chance to talk to with Cleo last night?" I ask, sliding my hand up her thigh, dragging the hem of the dress with it. *No underwear, which means she definitely wants attention.*

"I read to her and the other girls as they were falling asleep, so I didn't get the chance before she was out." Xoe makes a little noise in her throat as I find her clit with my fingers, slowly rubbing in circles as she spreads her thighs for me. "B-but I think she felt better after he left. She wasn't upset at bedtime."

"Hmm..." I acknowledge that I heard her as I think over the information. Even as I think, I'm steadily pleasuring her, which has caught the attention of a few of the kids on the floor, both the older and younger ones, but we don't hide these things. It's helpful for the younger ones to see what will happen when they're old enough... to see how good loving your family can be.

But my mind is focused elsewhere. I'm thinking about Cleo, her response to Richter's ploy to make her remember him. Did she remember? Was she upset by his presence, or the memories themselves?

When she was little, she used to wake up crying for her mama, and I did my best, along with Xoe, to make her feel loved and welcome. Eventually she stopped waking up searching for her mama and started calling for me. Her sweet little voice crying out 'Daddy' from the hallway still makes my heart warm, and if Richter thinks he can come between us he's going to learn a hard lesson that I know Luke never taught him.

Love always wins.

Xoe's hips are rocking on my lap, her ass waking up my dick with each wiggle, and I squeeze her hip with my other hand to hold her in place.

"You know I want to make you feel good, baby girl," I whisper against her shoulder, and she whines as she nods, seeking her pleasure as I dip two fingers inside before returning them to her clit. "I'm proud of you for seeking me out instead of touching yourself."

"Thank you, Daddy," she says on a gasp, moaning softly, and I can't hide my grin as the room has gone quiet while they watch. Picking up speed, I listen to every panting breath, each little sound, and I know she's close. I know what each of my older children sound like when they're close to bliss, and I'm always happy to take them there.

A second later, Xoe arches, moaning louder as she soaks my fingers, and I thrust them inside her, moving in and out to help her ride the orgasm.

"Daddy," she murmurs, breathing hard as she shifts on my lap, coming down from the high with a soft hum in her chest. "Thank you so much."

"You're welcome, baby girl." I tap her hip, helping her to stand up. She glances down at my lap, but I just smile and tilt my head toward the kitchen. "We need to start lunch soon."

"Okay, Daddy," she answers, her cheeks still flushed pink, her face glowing with love for me. "Will sandwiches work?"

"Sounds wonderful," I approve, watching her as she bounces into the kitchen. I lick my fingers clean, enjoying her taste, but when I look back down, Heather is watching me from a few feet away. I have to chuckle as the blush in her cheeks tells me that more than just Xoe is feeling needy today. Moira's words come back to haunt me, and I'm about to tell my girl she can get in my lap when I hear a car outside.

Standing, I adjust myself in my jeans, looking out the front windows to see Richter's truck. The sight brings a smile to my face, a warm rush through my chest as I realize there are two figures in the cab of the truck.

He brought Skylar.

"Sweetheart, I promise I'll show you my love later. But right now, I need to welcome Richter and his sister to our home." Cupping Heather's cheek, I can see the disappointment in her eyes, but she nods.

"Okay, Daddy. Do you need help?"

"No, but your mama would probably appreciate some help with lunch. Tell her we have two extra sandwiches to make."

"On it!" Climbing to her feet, Heather flashes a smile before going to obey me. It gives me a rush as I move to the front door, glancing behind me to see who's in the house.

"Casey!" I call out, but it's Owen who looks up at me.

"He's out back chopping firewood, Daddy."

"Run and get him for me, okay, son?" I ask, and Owen seems thrilled by the idea of abandoning his schoolwork to run outside. He's already on his feet and hurrying to the backdoor when I add, "Then you come back here and finish your studies."

"Yes, Daddy," he answers, his shoulders dipping a little as he shoves his feet into his boots and tugs on his coat.

I open the door just as Richter and Skylar are shutting their doors, and I feel my cock twitch as I see her.

She's pretty. Very pretty, and I'm not surprised that some of her features resemble my own girls as she gets closer. The only thing marring her perfect face is a slight swelling of her lower lip, a shadow around it that might be a bruise.

He wouldn't.

My eyes drift to Richter, and I can see he's come prepared for a fight. Chest puffed up, back tense and straight, but I don't give him the opportunity to confront me.

"Richter, Skylar, I'm so glad you came today. Come in," I welcome them as I step back, holding the door open for them.

Skylar glances at him, and I can see some of the fire has gone out of Richter as he leads the way inside, his sister on his heels. Her eyes go wide as she sees the little ones on the floor, just like Richter's did.

"This is your family," I say, smiling warmly at her when she looks up at me. "And we're so glad you're here."

EIGHTEEN

Skylar

My family.

I take in his words, his smile, his demeanor, and everything I can in the single moment that I hold his eyes.

I don't want Richter to get upset so I know that I can't look anyone here in the eye for too long.

I take a deep breath as I tuck a strand of hair behind my ear and shift a step closer to Richter. As of yet, he hasn't made a move to let go of my hand. I'm his property—that's just how it is with the Greene men.

But this Bryden, there's something different about him. I can see Dad in the way he holds himself, with pride and strength, but that's where it ends. No one in his home shows any signs of fear, nor do they look like they want to flee. The small children are all busy with their schoolwork, while the older ones closer to our ages, are helping them or doing chores. But they're all chatting happily, and I hear someone laugh from deeper in the house. It seems so... normal.

How can he possibly be a Greene, then?

Richter gives my hand a squeeze and I steal a glance at

him. He can see the uncertainty as it settles over me that, maybe, this man isn't who he says he is.

"Wow, there's a lot of you," I finally say with a nervous smile. Richter squeezes my hand a little too tightly, and when I glance at him, he shakes his head at me with stern eyes.

Just like Dad.

"And it looks like it just got a little bigger," Bryden replies with the same warm smile still on his face.

"Mm," I mumble as I lower my eyes to the floor.

"You two are just in time to join us for lunch. Sandwiches okay?" he asks as he motions for us to follow him into the kitchen.

There's a girl standing there with her back to us making the largest pile of sandwiches I've ever seen. In a weird way, it makes me grateful that it's just Richter and I because there's no way I would have as much patience as she seemingly does right now.

"Xoe," Bryden greets the girl. "Sweetheart, say hello to Richter and Skylar."

When she turns around, I feel a pang of jealousy swell inside of me. She greets us with the same smile as her... um, father? And she's damn beautiful too.

It's when I take a step closer to Richter and manage to wriggle my hand from his grip to slide it around his waist. Her eyes take us both in, but they linger longer on him, and while I'm not entirely happy about the situation our legacy has bestowed upon us, I won't let him leave me.

Not for her.

Not for anyone.

But my brother glances down at me with a curious smile on his face, then drapes an arm around my shoulders before he turns his grin back toward Bryden and Xoe.

"So, we meet again," he jokes lamely with her.

She returns his grin and nods as Bryden watches the exchange from where he's now leaning against the counter.

When our eyes meet again, I bite my lower lip and look away.

He's so much older than us, almost Dad's age when we were born, that I find it hard to believe that even Luke Greene was able to keep a secret like this for so damn long.

"Lunch will be ready soon, Daddy," Xoe says to Bryden after she tears her eyes away from Richter. "I'll have them on the table shortly."

"Thank you, Xoe," he replies with a smile as he pushes himself away from the counter. She takes a step toward him, anticipating a reward of sorts, and when he gives her arm a squeeze, I can see the hope deflate inside of her like a balloon.

Maybe he's a Greene after all, I think with an eyeroll as we follow him into his family's living room.

"My son Casey will be along shortly. He's just finishing up his chores then he'll join us," Bryden tells us with a smile as the rest of us sit down to eat. I glance around the table, stealing quick glances at everyone, wondering how it's possible to be so damn happy, but sigh when I notice Cleo isn't here.

"Ah," Bryden says with a knowing nod when he notices my demeanor. "Heather, can you please fetch Sierra and Cleo? They've got sandwiches waiting for them here."

I look excitedly at Richter who takes a deep breath when our eyes meet. I can see the hope starting to shine in his eyes and I know that we're sharing the same thought.

Maybe if she sees us both together, she'll remember.

He rests a hand on my thigh as the Heather girl gets to her feet and leaves the room.

"Skylar?" Bryden begins thoughtfully. "Tell me something about yourself. I'm very interested in getting to know my family, and I hope you feel the same way."

I turn my attention toward him as I push my plate away and fold my arms on the tabletop. I can see the momentary flicker of anger in him at me rejecting his 'lunch' but when he clears his throat, it's gone as quickly as it showed up.

"There's not much to say if I'm being honest. It's just Richter and me. We live in our Dad's house and have been alone for a lot longer than I think either of us care to be."

I don't mean to sound as snappy and bitchy as I do with my last words, but if Cleo recognizes me, I have every intention of getting her out of this home. I won't let her come with me and Richter, but maybe I can find a place where people like her are all the same and she can be taken care of by someone with the qualifications to do so.

Bryden raises his cup to his lips, his eyes holding mine the entire time, and when he sets it down, I can see the flicker of Dad again.

It seems like there's a war raging inside of him at my behavior and if Luke wins, we're all fucked.

Which, of course, happens to be the Greene family way.

"So, Bryden," I reply in a mockingly cheerful voice. "Tell me something about yourself. I mean if we're family and all, you should at the very least be willing to share. In every sense of the word, of course."

He lets out a good-natured chuckle as he sets his cup down, and with the shake of his head, picks up his sandwich and takes another bite.

I grit my teeth but do my best not to show my frustration on the surface.

Once he sets his sandwich back down on his plate, he reaches for a napkin to wipe his mouth. This game of cat and mouse I intended on playing isn't working out as well as I thought it would. I keep dangling the damn bait in his face and while he shows signs of falling for it, he's managed to keep his composure throughout.

Fine, I think, *let me try something else.*

"So, who's your mother?" I ask him in the same mocking manner. "It can't be Darby. Know how I know? Because our mother would never leave any of her children behind."

Bryden smiles as he leans over and whispers something into Xoe's ear before leaning back in his chair again. Still no answer, no slip of the tongue—no sign of Luke fucking Greene.

"What happened there?" he asks, nodding at my lip, causing me to blush and sink in my seat.

"She fell," Richter intercedes quickly.

"Oh yeah?" Bryden presses.

I nod as I turn my attention toward the sandwich and pull the plate back to me. I already know that this is going to taste like shit for no other reason than I spoiled my own damn appetite by being mouthy with the man of the house.

Something that Dad would never have stood for.

"Hey, Daddy, sorry that took so long."

I turn my eyes toward the sound of the voice I have yet to become acquainted with, and swallow hard. The young man that enters the room is beautiful, slightly out of breath, and sweaty from whatever efforts his chores caused him. He has his shirt off, the fabric tucked into the waistband of his jeans, and as he runs a hand back through his sweat-slicked hair, I watch intently as every muscle of his taut stomach contracts, then eases from the motion.

"It's fine, son," Bryden tells him as he raises a hand. "This is Skylar," he says gesturing toward me. "And she's here for lunch."

The young man turns his eyes toward me, and when they settle, I can feel my face burn crimson. I think Richter notices too because he gingerly ribs me with his elbow, but I keep my eyes trained on my lap.

I don't want to see the disappointment on his face that I'm looking at another man the way he wishes I would look at him. I don't want to know that I've hurt him by doing so because the ache in my heart will be too much to bear.

"I'm Casey," he says, and I steal a glance to look up at him again. His lips begin to slip into a grin as he turns his eyes back toward his father, then to me again. *Deep breaths, Skylar.* "You're Richter's sister?"

I take a deep breath, clear my throat, and turn my face toward him. "Yes. And Cleo's. Any idea where she may be?"

Casey chuckles as he removes his shirt from where it's tucked and pulls it over his head. "Probably with Sierra."

"Who?" I ask in confusion.

"Sierra is my daughter," Bryden explains from where he sits. "Just like Luke left Cleo in my care to be. She's happy, fed, and loved here, Skylar. And you can be too."

I turn my head sharply toward him. "I want to see my sister," I tell him stubbornly.

He shakes his head for a second before he holds his hands up in concession and looks at Casey.

"Take her to the girls' room, son," he instructs him. "I'm sure you'll be able to bring Sierra and Cleo to the table faster if two of you are looking instead of one."

Casey walks over to where I'm sitting with Richter. The smell of him is intoxicating—sweat mixed with the scent of freshly chopped wood.

He nods at my brother before he turns his attention to me and holds out a hand.

"Come on," he says with a smile. "Let's see where the girls are hiding. I bet it will be fun."

I look over at Richter, not for permission but to let him know that I'll be okay. Maybe we'll find Cleo and maybe it's all a game, but at the end of the day at least we'll have each other and that's all that matters.

Isn't it?

NINETEEN

Casey

Daddy winks at me as I lead Skylar out of the kitchen and across the living room, and I feel honored that he trusts me with her. She's beautiful, and as I slow to a stop outside of the bedroom Cleo, Sierra, and Moira share, I take a minute to look at her.

"What is it?" she asks, nervously tucking her hair behind her ear as she breaks our contact. I don't try to hold onto her hand, even though I want to. Her skin is soft, and I like the feel of it against mine.

Skylar is new, but she's family.

Which means I'm supposed to take care of her.

"Your lip..." I start to ask about it, but she turns away, shrugging.

"I fell. It's fine. Is Cleo in here?" she asks, reaching for the doorknob, but I touch her shoulder and she doesn't open it.

"You know that family has to protect family, right?" I smile when she glances at me, and I feel it stretch as her eyes avoid mine and move down, over my shirt that clings to my sweat-coated chest and stomach. My sisters like my body, they like to run their fingers over the ridges of my abs, and I gently turn Skylar so she's facing me and not the bedroom door. "If you got hurt on my watch, I'd never forgive myself, but I'd take care of you until you were better."

Her pretty eyes lift to mine again, lips parting like she wants to speak, but she doesn't.

"Does Richter take care of you?" I whisper, letting her know that her answer can be our secret, but all I get is a blush rising in her cheeks. She's so pretty. Shy in a way that my sisters aren't, and it makes me want to draw her out of her shell. "You're safe here, Skylar. I promise."

"I want to see Cleo," she whispers, looking at the door again, and I back off. I want her to believe me. I want her to know that I'd never hurt her, because I'm pretty sure that Richter did—which means he's not a real man.

A punishment would be a strap across her ass, or time alone in the closet... never hitting. *We never hit our family*, that's something we teach even the youngest in the house.

"Go on then." I struggle to keep the smile on my face while a low, burning rage builds in my stomach. As she opens the door to go inside, I'm struck by the visual of embedding the axe from outside in Richter's back. If I did that... he'd never be able to lay a hand on her again.

"Cleo?" Skylar's soft voice says, and I hear the girls giggling as I finally follow her inside, shutting the door behind me. Heather is sitting on the floor outside their blanket fort, looking exasperated.

"They're in their hideaway, and they *don't want to come out for lunch*," Heather says, lacing her voice with friendly irritation as she looks up at Skylar and then me, a smile forming on her lips. "Oh Cleooooo, you have someone here who wants to talk to you."

"We can't leave! We're princesses and we were locked inside by a witch!" Sierra argues, more giggles escaping as I grin and lean back against the door.

"Yeah! It's a curse!" Cleo adds.

"Oh no, well... do you think we can break the curse?" Heather asks, waving Skylar closer with a smile.

"It's strong magic," Sierra explains through the layers of fabric.

Skylar hesitates, a slight frown on her face, but she slowly moves forward, moving to kneel beside Heather when my sister pats the floor. Leaning closer to the place where the blankets separate, Skylar beckons our sister again. "Cleo, it's Skylar. Your sister. Will you come out?"

"We can't!" Both girls answer, still laughing in their sweet voices.

Heather leans over, whispering something in Skylar's ear, and then she sits back, motioning toward her.

"Um..." Skylar swallows, toying with her hair again. "I brought some magic dust from my house. It's where Cleo, Richter, and I used to live together... when Cleo was little. Do you think that might break the curse?"

"Oooo, maybe!" Sierra answers, but Cleo is quiet.

"Okay, well, Skylar is sprinkling the magic dust all over the castle, and—wow! It looks like the spell is breaking!" Heather is using the same voice she uses with the younger kids, and it makes me proud of her. She's such a good mama, as all of my sisters are, and I wonder why Skylar doesn't have any kids yet.

They would have brought them if they did.

"It worked?" Sierra asks, peeking out of the blanket fort, and Heather lifts one of the blankets with a dramatic gasp.

"It did! Amazing!" Heather laughs, squeezing Skylar's

arm. "Apparently Skylar is very good with magic spells, and now you both can come eat lunch with us."

Sierra crawls out, her eyes finding me against the wall, and I can see the need lingering in her gaze as she looks me over.

"Cleo?" Skylar calls again, leaning into the little fort. "Can you come out?"

"I don't want to," Cleo answers, her voice turning sour.

"But it's been a long time since I've seen you, and I really want to," Skylar pleads. "Please?"

There's no answer, but the edge of the blanket shifts and Cleo peeks out. Skylar covers her mouth, her shoulders pulling in, and I feel tension rush through me as I realize she's trying not to cry.

"You have magic dust?" Cleo asks quietly, and Skylar shrugs before nodding a bit as she sniffles.

"I did, we... we used it break the spell." Brushing her hands under her eyes, Skylar tries to smile. "Do you recognize me, Cleo?"

Cleo's face pinches, eyes narrowing. "I don't know."

"Skylar is your sister," I confirm, and Cleo looks over at me, listening because she knows I'd never lie to her.

"Like Sierra? And Heather?" Cleo clarifies, and I remember what Daddy told me about Cleo when she showed up here. That his Daddy brought her because she needed a family to love her—and we have. I was a year older than her when she showed up at breakfast one morning. She cried a lot at first, and I did everything I could to make her feel better. I let her play with all my toys, I let her hold the book when Xoe was teaching us to read. If anything, Sierra and Heather are more like family to Cleo than Skylar is, but I won't say that.

It isn't Skylar's fault her Daddy couldn't take care of so many kids.

"Yes, Skylar is your sister just like Sierra and Heather. We're all family," I confirm, and Skylar gives me an odd look before turning toward Cleo again.

"Do you remember me?" she asks, and I can tell she's struggling not to cry.

"I don't know!" Cleo snaps, crossing her arms. Then she looks at Heather with a pout firmly on her face. "Isn't it lunchtime?"

"It is," Heather says, pushing herself to her feet as she gives Skylar an apologetic smile. "Let's all go eat. Xoe and I made sandwiches!"

"I like sandwiches!" Cleo announces, bouncing to her feet to grab Sierra's hand. I open the door, letting them rush out, and Heather follows quickly on their heels. Skylar is slower to stand though, and I walk over to her as she gets to her feet.

"It's okay, she'll remember you," I tell her, reaching to brush the tears off her cheek, but she turns her head away. I can tell she's in pain, that Cleo's answers hurt her feelings, and so I do what I would do for any of my sisters. I open my arms wide and ask, "Do you want a hug?"

Skylar's face snaps up to look at me, surprise on her face, but she eventually shakes her head. "I-I can't."

"Why not? We're family, aren't we?" I gently touch her arms, nudging her toward me with a light tug. "What good is family if we can't comfort each other when we're upset?"

"I shouldn't," she whispers, but a second later she's against my chest, my arms wrapped around her back as I give her a light squeeze.

I know why she answered the way she did.

Richter.

"I'm sorry Cleo didn't recognize you, but I'm sure she will," I say, leaning my cheek against the top of Skylar's head as I sway with her a bit. The way her shaky exhale rushes over my chest has me imagining what she'd feel like in my bed. *Would she still be shy, or would she be like my sisters?* Grinning, I give her another comforting squeeze, her curves pressing against me as I add, "I think you'd be pretty hard to forget."

Skylar jerks back in my arms, and I immediately release her, holding onto my smile as she focuses on the wood under our feet.

"Sorry, I probably don't smell great," I say with a laugh. "I was chopping wood outside, and I got way too hot in my coat."

"No, you're fine," she says, running her hand under her nose, and I wonder if she's going to look at me again, but she's still too shy.

"It'll be okay, Skylar," I try to reassure her. "Let's go have lunch." Tilting my head toward the kitchen, I don't try to take her hand, but I do wait until she starts to follow me before I face forward again.

The table has rearranged a bit when we come back into the kitchen, and Daddy gives me a look that I can't quite figure out—but I don't get much of a chance.

"What were you doing?" Richter asks, glaring at Skylar who is returning to her seat meekly.

"Nothing," Skylar says, but when she sits down, I catch the flinch as Richter reaches over. I wish I was on that side of the tables so I could see what he's doing.

"We were breaking the witch's curse that was keeping Cleo and Sierra trapped in their castle," I answer, trying to keep my voice light as I take the last empty seat and relieve Moira of Weston so she can eat.

"Is that right?" Moira asks, grinning as she mouths a *'thank you'* at me. Weston immediately starts babbling at me, and I grin at him, adjusting his shirt which is getting a bit too small for him.

"Yes!" Sierra says through a mouthful of sandwich, and Daddy clears his throat. She immediately slaps her hand over it, chewing and swallowing before she looks up the table at him. "Sorry, Daddy."

"It's okay, baby. Just remember your manners."

"We were all lucky Skylar brought some magic dust with her," I continue, staring across the table at her and Richter. She's not touching her food, and neither is he, and I wonder what he's been whispering to her.

"Oh, really?" Daddy says, smiling. "What should you say to your sister for doing that, Cleo?"

"Thank you," Cleo says, glancing up at Skylar for a moment before tucking her chin to her chest.

"You're welcome," Skylar whispers, and Richter huffs.

"Skylar is your *real* sister, Cleo," he says, and I glare at him, but he's not looking at me. "Cleo, did you hear me?"

"Casey said she's my sister. Just like Sierra and all my sisters," Cleo replies, her face scrunching up, and I'm incredibly proud of her for defending our family.

"That's right," I confirm, watching Daddy's smile quirk up despite the tense hold of his jaw.

"That's *not* right," Richter growls. "Cleo shares the same mom and dad with Skylar and me. You remember Mom, right, Cleo?"

"I believe I asked you to be patient with her, Richter," Daddy says, and I know that hard edge to his voice. If Richter were anyone else, he'd already be in one of the bedrooms with Daddy and the strap. If it was up to me, he'd go straight to the closet... or outside.

"I have been patient!" Richter snaps, and Weston squirms in my lap, reacting to the raised voice.

"Richter, please," Skylar whispers, and he turns toward her, rage painting his face.

"It's time to come home, Cleo!" he says, practically shouting. "You belong with me and Skylar, back at our house."

Weston tries to grab for my sandwich, and I push the plate forward, tearing off a piece of bread for him to chew on.

"Cleo, look at me!" Richter yells, and Weston throws the bread onto the table, whining as he leans back, trying to wiggle out of my arms.

When I don't let him go, he sits up and smacks his little hand onto my chest. I catch it, holding him as I say, "No, Weston. We don't hit." Looking across the table, I meet Skylar's eyes a moment before I stare at Richter. "We *never* hit our family."

TWENTY

Skylar

Richter springs to his feet, fists balled at his sides. It seems Casey struck a chord with him in his controlled candor, and my brother isn't going to stand for it.

"What happens in *our* home, under *my* roof, is none of your business," he seethes at him before he turns his eyes toward Bryden. *"You* are not our family; I don't care who you say your father is. You haven't proven shit to me, and my sister belongs with us."

"Richter," I hiss at him. "Calm down."

I mean for my words to come out in urgency—in hope that he'll understand that I'm not speaking down to him but rather begging him to keep his temper in check. He shoots me a sharp look and I slump a little further into my chair. Casey hands the child he's holding to the girl next to him and gets to his feet as well.

"That's enough of that," Bryden says loudly from the head of the table. "Everyone take a deep breath and let's try this again."

I reach up and lay a hand on my brother's arm, but he shakes it away violently. It's not Richter Greene standing beside me anymore, it's Luke and only God can help us out of this now.

Bryden lets out a sigh, as neither Casey nor Richter show any signs of backing down, and he gets to his feet. I sink further still as he makes his way around the table, stopping behind my chair and resting a hand on my shoulder.

"Richter, you have to understand that Casey is just protective of his family—that's how all of my children were raised. Casey," he continues as he turns his attention to the young man. "You know I don't allow fighting in my house. Please take a seat and finish your lunch."

"Get up," Richter says through gritted teeth, and until he looks at me, I wasn't sure who he was talking to. I glance up at Bryden feeling apologetic and a little scared, but my brother is right—he *hasn't* proven that he's our brother so there's no need to be cordial any longer.

"Come on," Richter says as he takes my hand in his. I let him lead me around the table to where Cleo is sitting, still refusing to look up, and seemingly afraid of everything that's transpired in front of her.

When we reach her, we take a spot on either side of her and crouch down.

"Cleo," Richter begins in a soft tone. "Do you remember Darby?"

She closes her eyes tightly and shakes her head vehemently, but I know she's lying. That's how she used to react when we were younger, and Dad would ask us who had 'fucked up today.'

"Honey," I tell her gently as I rest a hand on her leg. "The last time you saw us was right before Dad took you into town. You were supposed to help him with some shopping. Do you remember that?"

A tear rolls down her face as she shakes her head again and it makes me wonder if she's acting like she doesn't remember because she really doesn't, or if she's trying to block out the memory because Dad did something to her on that trip.

It's late afternoon and we're still in Bryden's home. He somehow managed to diffuse the tension between Casey and Richter by asking to talk to them in 'the other room like men.'

When they reemerged, my brother was still angry but way more compliant and Casey seemed to be in good spirits again.

I passed the time by helping the older of the girls help the younger ones with their schoolwork since Heather ended up taking Sierra and Cleo back to their room.

Instead of being the hero that broke the witch's curse, I became worse in her eyes than any monster she could have ever imagined.

"Skylar come talk to me," Bryden says as he enters the room. When he sees the look on my face, he smiles and holds a hand up. "The boys will be fine. They've come to an agreement."

Curiosity takes hold of me, but I've already pressed the man of the house too much—acted too rudely to ask him what the agreement is. I'm sure he'll tell me when he feels the time is right and who knows when that will be?

"Sure," I reply as I get to my feet and follow him back into the kitchen.

Xoe is currently cleaning up, but when her father tells

her that she's excused, she leaves us alone without a word or glance.

"What's up?" I ask him nervously as I cross my arms loosely over my chest.

"I can't help but feel like we got off on the wrong foot," he begins with a chuckle. "Neither of you seem to believe that I'm your brother and you've asked for proof. Is my family not proof enough? Isn't this the same thing that Luke has done for generations? You see, we have different mothers, and now that you and Richter have shown up, I wouldn't be surprised if more of us are wandering around. But the only family that matters to me is the family that I can see—that I can touch," he finishes as he reaches a hand forward, brushing my hair behind my ear.

I turn my face away from him, because in this moment, I *do* feel like he could be telling the truth.

My mind is more muddled than Cleo's. I don't know who's telling the truth anymore, I think miserably.

"I don't want you to be unhappy here—or Richter. I want to show you both that you can love your family and be loved in return. Not everything that our father did to his children should be carried down. And that includes this," he says, moving his hand down to my lower lip. "This is a Greene trait that doesn't exist in my home, nor should it in yours."

"I fell," I tell him again in a shaky voice as I pull away from his touch. "That's all that happened."

Bryden clears his throat and takes a deep breath. "I'd like you to spend some time with Casey. Richter agreed to it, so there's no worry about what he'll say, okay? Just go out back with him and have a talk. Find out how our family works, and you'll understand how and why everyone here is happy, loved, and cared for."

I raise my eyes to his and do my best to control the tremble that's going through my body. I don't want to spend time with anyone under his fucking roof unless it's my little sister, but it seems that he has hurdles that need to be leaped before he gives in.

If he gives in.

"And if I do this, will you let me spend time with Cleo? Alone?" I ask in a shaky voice.

"I promise," he replies, a smile slipping over his lips. "Casey!"

I jump slightly at the sound of his voice because I hadn't expected it to be so strong this loud.

"Yes, Daddy?" he asks from behind me.

"Take Skylar out back. Have a little chat with her about how things work here and see if you can't put her mind at ease."

"Sure thing," he replies enthusiastically. I feel his presence when he comes to stand behind me, and when he leans down and whispers into my ear, I wonder if I'll actually believe anything he has to say to me.

"Damn, I forgot to stack the wood," he mumbles under his breath once we get outside. "Gimme a sec?"

I nod and sit on the back step as he wanders over to the pile of wood he chopped earlier in the day. I tuck my hands beneath my thighs as he meticulously makes a neat little pyramid out of them.

When he's finally done, he pulls his shirt up to his nose, makes a face at me, then smiles when I giggle shyly.

"Can I ask you something?" he says as he sits down on

the spot next to me. I shrug and glance at him expectantly. "Did Richter do that to your face?"

I take a deep breath and let it out in a heavy sigh. That seems to be the question of the day and no one wants to believe that I got these bumps and bruises from falling.

"You can tell me," he urges gently as he rests a hand on my thigh.

"I made him angry," I confess quietly. "But it was my fault. I'm not his punching bag, you know? It's just that sometimes I push him too much and that's when the Dad in him comes out."

"I'd never lay a hand on you. No matter how angry you made me, though I don't think you ever could," he says thoughtfully. "But if it's okay with you, I'd like to have a talk with him—man to man—so that he doesn't do this again."

"No, it's okay," I reply quickly. "It's very few and far between that it happens."

"It shouldn't happen at all, Skylar," he tells me softly as he inches his hand to the inside of my leg. "Daddy doesn't allow any of us to hit each other. No matter how angry we get, everything can be talked out. And, honestly, there's never really a time I remember being so angry that the thought even crossed my mind. Daddy is a great man—you just have to give his rules a chance is all. You can be as happy as the rest of us."

I shake my head and blow out my breath again. "I don't belong here, Casey. Neither does Richter or Cleo. I get that we're probably going about this the wrong way, but she's our sister and she belongs with us in *our* home."

I doubt that if I tell him of my intentions once we get her out of here, he'd be willing to even listen anymore. Hell, he'd probably tell Bryden, who would no doubt tell Richter, and then where would I be?

At the bottom of the oubliette where all disobedient Greene women go.

"Can I ask you one more question?" he asks, scooting a little closer to me, the tips of his fingers brushing the crotch of my jeans. I turn to look at him—his eyes, his lips, the way he brushes them quickly with his tongue—and I nod. "How do you show Richter your love?"

I blanch.

I wasn't expecting that, and quite honestly it isn't something I feel comfortable talking about, because while I *do* love my brother... it's not in actions or words. It's simply in the beating of both our hearts that came from the same parents.

It's because I have to love him, but it's never how he *wants* me to.

"I tell him," I reply in a shaky tone as Casey leans forward and brushes his lips against mine. I suck in a breath as need takes over sense and I lean into his gentle kiss.

He chuckles slightly when we break apart and slips an arm around my waist, using his other hand to pop the button on my jeans. Then he slowly pulls my zipper down and strokes his fingertips across my underwear.

"Is this okay, Skylar?" he asks, his lips brushing against my neck. "Is this what you want too?"

I close my eyes and nod.

To think that I could be with a man that *isn't* Richter is scandalous to say the least, but this feels so right that it can't be wrong.

"Let me show you how family is supposed to love each other," he whispers as he slips his hand inside my underwear and uses his forefinger to circle my clit.

I take in a sharp breath as I lean into Casey, resting my forehead against the side of his face. He tightens his grip around me, snaking his hand up my shirt, holding me close, brushing my nipple over the bra, then squeezing my breast tightly.

"Does this feel good, Skylar?" he asks, and I nod as my hips begin to roll slowly against the sensations he's sending through me. "How about this?" he whispers, slipping a finger inside me.

My mouth is open as my breathing becomes ragged and Casey chuckles. He brushes his lips against my forehead as he begins to thrust his fingers in and out of me as best as he can.

I grip his leg, digging my nails into the fabric of his jeans, doing my best not to make noise.

I don't want anyone to hear me because then they'll stop us, and this feels too good to fucking stop.

"Good girl," he whispers as he moves his fingers back to my clit. He presses down hard, gives it a pinch, then begins to circle it again until my breathing becomes labored, until the feeling is too much—until my body betrays its loyalty to Richter's touch and I bite down hard on my lower lip to keep from moaning out loud as pleasure rushes through me.

Casey gently takes his hands out of my shirt and jeans but keeps me held tightly.

"This is why we're so happy, Skylar. Because we know how family should be loved. Isn't that something worth fighting for?" Another soft kiss against my hair. "It's why Daddy won't give up Cleo so quickly—why he won't give up on you and Richter. You deserve to be loved, and we can do that for you both. *I* can do that for you."

I pull away from Casey and give his hand a gentle shove before I reach down and pull the zipper of my jeans back up. I don't know what I want, but the last thing I need is a

Greene Family pile-on, and that seems to be what he's suggesting.

As he gets to his feet next to me, I shake my head at him and turn to walk back into the house when I see Bryden and Richter standing there, staring at us.

Bryden with a proud look on his face and Richter looking betrayed.

Did they see what just happened?

TWENTY-ONE

Bryden

Skylar has a beautiful flush on her face, and I recognize the look Casey gives me just before his face goes blank. Just like I'd hoped, Casey has started to show her what it's like to be loved, *truly* loved.

Not Luke Greene's version of love.

Everyone is looking at Richter, and I reach over to rest my hand on his shoulder. A fatherly gesture that he doesn't immediately shrug off, but I acknowledge that has more to do with his concerns over Casey and Skylar spending time together than his acceptance of me or my family. "Richter was just telling me how he has a computer with the internet, and that he taught himself how to use it to find Cleo."

"Yeah," Richter mumbles, finally shifting his shoulder out from under my hand. "I noticed you guys don't even have a TV."

"A TV?" Casey repeats, looking at me, and I smile at him.

"Something that other families have to entertain them. From what I understand, it's the same with a computer." I smile as I tuck my thumbs into my pockets. "We just don't need those things."

"Your kids might disagree," Richter says, side-eyeing me, and I fight the urge to grab him by the back of the neck and shake him for questioning me. *That* is what Luke would have done. Instead, I simply shrug my shoulders.

"Maybe." I lean against the doorframe, smiling at the pretty pair my son makes with Richter's sister. "Skylar, what do you think of the computer?"

Her eyes widen slightly, looking between me and Richter with a vague sheen of panic. "I... um..."

"Skylar doesn't use the computer," Richter answers, and I chuckle.

"Well, then I guess it's not that necessary." I turn to face him as I glance back at the kids getting their outside clothes on. "But I am glad you used it to find us."

"Daddy! Up!" Embry says, running over to me, and I scoop her into my arms, settling her onto my hip as I adjust the puffy coat on her shoulders. "Play in snow?" she asks, pointing outside, and I nod.

"Absolutely! We just need to wait for your brothers and sisters."

"Nooooo!" she whines, squirming as she reaches for the doorway. "Ou'side!"

"Patience, baby girl," I say, bouncing her a little as I look at Skylar. She's curious about the girl in my arms, and I go with my gut as I walk onto the porch and hand her Embry. "Here. Go with Skylar, she's your sister. She'll take you outside with Casey."

"I—" Skylar stumbles over her words as she grabs onto Embry, shifting my daughter to her hip instinctively.

"Will you and Casey take her to play in the snow? The others will be out in just a minute."

"RACE YOU!" Gavin shouts, charging past us with Owen on his heels.

"Not fair!" Owen whines as Gavin runs full speed and leaps off the porch.

Chuckling, I tilt my chin toward the backyard. "Go on, I think you'll enjoy having a little fun."

"Snooow!" Embry whines, leaning toward the backyard while she tugs at Skylar's shirt.

"Richter, if you wouldn't mind staying inside with me so we can keep talking?" I smile at him, but I can tell he's anxious. He doesn't like being separated from Skylar, but he needs to learn to trust us.

We're family. Skylar couldn't be safer.

"About what?" he asks, and Casey reads my mind as he guides Skylar and Embry off the porch as Heather and Moira head out past us. I nod at them and then turn inside, blocking Richter's line of sight as I close the door behind me.

"I want you to give us a chance, Richter. I understand what you want... for Cleo to return to your house with you and Skylar." A clatter comes from the hallway, followed by a round of raucous giggles, and I chuckle as Sierra and Cleo leave their fortress to join the family for outside time. They race each other to the remaining shoes and coats by the backdoor, hopping as they pull on their boots quickly.

"Cleo, I was looking for you," Richter says, reaching for his sister, but she's too wound up to stay still for him. "Can you stay here for a minute?"

"It's outside time!" Cleo says, shoving her arms into her coat, and there's no ignoring the round of her belly in the shirt she has on now. She must have grown too warm playing in her room. "Sierra and me are going to have a snowball fight with the boys. You can't be on our team because you're a boy, but you can play with Gavin and Owen."

"Maybe in a bit, sweetheart," I answer her, and she just shrugs, pushing Sierra toward the door, and they're gone in a flash.

"Why do you keep trying to separate us?" Richter snaps, facing off with me, and I sigh, pointing out the window.

"Come here and watch them." Looking out, I can see the kids already starting their snowball fight. Running and playing. Skylar has put Embry down in the snow, but she's hovering near her, watching, and I can tell she'd be a wonderful mother.

One of the boys lands a snowball on her back, and Skylar turns, surprised, but then she smiles... and it's radiant. She laughs, reaching down to make a snowball to toss back at them, and even though she misses, I feel warm inside as I see her laugh. Glancing at Richter, his furrowed brow and pinched mouth, I can tell he hasn't seen her like this in a long time.

"I'm not trying to separate you two, Richter," I continue. "In fact, what I'm *trying* to do is show you how welcome you and Skylar would be here. How happy you could be here... just like Cleo is."

"Cleo would be happier at home with me and Skylar."

"Really?" I ask, turning my gaze out the window again. "Here she has brothers and sisters to play with, a big family who love and care for her. And Sierra is her best friend. They've been inseparable since Luke left her here with me." I point out at them, the two girls bent down in the snow to form more snowballs. Grinning and laughing loudly. "I know you love your sisters, Richter, and I know you wouldn't want to hurt Cleo."

"Of course not!"

"Well, taking her away from Sierra would hurt her." Looking at him, I shrug. "She's been here for thirteen years, Richter, and while I hope she remembers the connection she had with you and Skylar... that won't erase the bonds she has here. I don't want her to have to choose."

Richter opens his mouth to speak, but he shuts it again, glaring out the window as he thinks, and I give him some space. Turning, I see Brinnah setting up the foldable fencing that Damon helped me make years ago. She blocks off the fireplace, leaning it against my chair so that the little ones are directed toward the couch and back into the living room.

"Do you need any help, Brinnah?" I ask, and she smiles at me as she lifts Weston out of his crib to play on the floor.

"No, Daddy. I'm good!" She takes out Lissa next, bouncing her on her hip for a second. "I have a feeling Lissa is going to walk today. Abigail definitely wants her sister to walk!"

Abigail babbles at her mama, blowing spit bubbles from the crib beside Lissa's, reaching as Brinnah grins at her.

"That would be wonderful," I say, sensing that Richter is watching us now. "If she starts to walk, definitely call for me. Richter and I are going to talk to Xoe, okay?"

"Okay, Daddy," Brinnah says, taking Abigail out and putting her on the floor with her siblings.

"I want to go outside with Cleo and Skylar," Richter argues, but I'm still between him and the door.

"Let's talk with Xoe real quick, then we'll go out and you can show off your snowball skills." Smiling at him, straining to be patient, I gesture toward the kitchen and eventually he relents. Muttering under his breath as he walks ahead of me.

"Hey Daddy," Xoe says, leaning away from the fridge to smile at us. "I'm just taking inventory of what we have, adding to the shopping list."

"Anything we're short on?" I ask, and her head tilts as she looks at the notepad on the counter.

"Eggs," she answers, planting a hand on her hip. "You know, if we could get some chickens this Spring, I think we'd save a lot on those."

"Good idea," I acknowledge, nudging Richter gently. "Maybe Richter here could help me and Casey build a coop for them."

"I don't know how to do that," he answers, straightening his back as soon as the admission is out of his mouth.

"That's okay. We can teach you." Beckoning Xoe, I tilt my head toward her room. "Come talk to us, sweetheart. You can finish the inventory later."

"Okay, Daddy," she says, shutting the fridge to join us.

I point off the kitchen at the doorway just past the second table. "I added that room on myself years ago. We needed the space."

"Obviously," Richter grumbles, but when Xoe reaches for his hand his eyes widen.

"Come on," she says, leading him to her room as I follow behind them. Xoe takes him right to her bed, sitting down on the edge and pulling him to sit beside her. The look on his face confirms what I thought yesterday—he likes Xoe.

He may not like me, or Casey, or trust any of us, but Xoe has his attention.

"I was hoping you'd help me talk to Richter about how we show our love," I say, and Xoe smiles at me before she turns to Richter.

"It's not that complicated. We love everyone equally, share it whenever we can, and we make sure no one feels left behind." Reaching up, Xoe runs her hand along his jaw. "You're very handsome," she whispers in her soft voice.

"Th-thanks," he replies, and I can see that he's tense. Unsure. It's always this way the first time the boys get the opportunity to love their family. I remember Wesley crying, and how Damon had kept his eyes closed so tight I thought he might never open them again. But when it was Casey's turn... Xoe had made it easier. He'd been nervous, just like Richter is now, but she'd soothed him. Shown him how he could share his love.

"I thought so yesterday too," Xoe continues, running her fingers over his lips. "But I didn't want to upset you."

Richter's hand lifts off his thigh, reaching for her, but he hesitates.

"It's okay," she encourages, taking his hand and bringing it to her waist. "I want you to."

"I don't—"

"There's nothing wrong with sharing your love, Richter," Xoe whispers, leaning in to kiss him softly, and I feel my cock twitch in my jeans as I watch her. She's such a good girl. The daughter I finally got right, the one who helped me build our family... and who might help me save the rest of it.

It takes a moment, but eventually Richter leans in, kissing her back, his hold on her waist tightening. She lets out a sweet sound as he pulls her closer, and in a smooth movement she swings her leg over him to straddle his lap on the bed—but Richter pulls back.

"I'm sorry... I thought..." Xoe's blonde hair tumbles over her shoulders as she looks down, but Richter's hands slowly shift to her hips, fisting the fabric of her dress. He doesn't speak, but, eventually, he does pull her closer, and their lips meet again. I know my girl isn't wearing any underwear, and she was needy this morning, so when she starts to rock her hips gently, I'm sure that Richter is responding.

"Please?" Xoe begs, a soft whine escaping her as Richter kisses down her throat.

"What?" Richter asks.

"I need you. Please?"

"You want me inside you?" There's an edge to his voice, hesitation or surprise, as his fingers squeeze her hips hard.

"Yes, please, Richter. I need it."

I stay silent, not even moving so that I don't distract them, but I hear the fastening on Richter's pants open and Xoe climbs off his lap for a moment. Standing directly in front of him, she pulls her dress over her head, and he shoves his pants down.

Their joint sighs as Xoe straddles him again, lowering herself slowly, are music to my ears. She's beautiful, the swell of her hips rolling as Richter runs his hands over her, and my girl keeps moving, just like I taught her.

I smile when Richter reaches between them, rubbing Xoe's clit to give her pleasure, because it gives me hope for him.

Maybe he knows how to show love despite being raised by Luke.

I linger beside the door until I hear Xoe cry out, her back arching, and Richter lifts her. Turning, he lays Xoe out on the bed, and he's back inside her a moment later. She wraps her legs around his hips, pulling him close, and I slip out the door as quietly as I can and join my family outside.

Everyone is still laughing and shouting, joyous as the snow starts to fall again. Big flakes floating down, making the world feel smaller. Casey sees me and tosses another snowball at one of his sisters before he hikes through the snow toward me.

"Well?" he asks, grinning, and I chuckle.

"Xoe is showing Richter how we share our love, and... I guess your discussion with Skylar went well earlier?"

"It did. She's shy though. Not like my other sisters. It's like she doesn't know if she wants to feel loved or not."

"Hmm..." I look out at her, finding her in the increasing snowfall with Embry on her hip, pointing up at the snowflakes. "Maybe she needs to know her sister is okay with it."

"Should I bring Cleo to my bed tonight, Daddy?" he asks, and I shake my head.

"No. If the snow keeps up, neither of them are going anywhere tonight. We'll let Skylar stay in Cleo's room, and I think if you visit Skylar there that things might go differently. Cleo and the other girls will encourage her."

"And if she doesn't want my love?" Casey looks at me, and I chuckle.

"She wants it, son. She's just waiting for permission to do what feels right." I pause, waving at Heather when she calls out to me. "And she's a smart girl. She'll know that Richter showed Xoe his love, and that will be all the permission she needs to accept yours."

TWENTY-TWO

Richter
_____

I betrayed Skylar.

The thought rings over and over in my head, accusing me of something that Dad would never have approved of. He's the only one that was ever able to do... things with us, and what I've just done with Xoe is something that he wouldn't forgive.

Fuck.

But how could something that feels so goddamn good be wrong? Isn't that why Dad did it to Mom so often? And our grandmother too?

I never did get the chance to meet her. Mom did once or twice when she was younger, but I wonder sometimes if she stayed with Dad willingly too.

Not that I think Darby did—I know she just wanted to keep us safe and happy, and that meant doing whatever he wanted her to.

Xoe looks at me expectantly when we're done, a smile on her face that Skylar's never given me afterward and I sit up, pulling my knees to my chest.

"Is everything okay?" she asks as she reaches over and lays a hand on my leg.

"Fine," I reply quietly as I move her hand away and get to my feet. I walk over to the window and glance out to see Skylar happily playing with the children. Maybe she'd be better off here too, with Cleo rather than with me, but then what would happen to the Greene Family legacy?

I promised Dad that I would continue it. It was the last thing I ever said to him before he took his last breath because it seemed to mean so much to him in his final moments.

A good son doesn't let his father down, and I'm damn determined to be the best son I can be. It's what he would expect of me.

Xoe's soft hands make me jump as she rests them on my back, her cheek filling in the small gap they make against my skin and I sigh.

"Listen," I say when I finally manage to tear my eyes away from Skylar. "That was great; it really was. But you're not who I'm supposed to be with. Dad didn't know you and I'm pretty sure if he did, he wouldn't have cared. The only children that ever mattered to him were the ones that came directly from him. You… you don't matter. Not under the rules we lived by."

Her lower lip begins to tremble dangerously as she takes a step back. It seems that this fucked up version of a Stepford Family can feel something besides constant joy after all.

"Why would you say that?" she inquires, her brow furrowing as a tear rolls down her cheek.

I take a deep breath as I square my shoulders, then look her straight in the eye. "You're no sister of mine. Your father wasn't Luke Greene—mine was. And Cleo's and Skylar's.

Maybe if you all weren't so busy touching each other, you'd understand how the real world works, girl."

That's all it takes for her to burst into tears. She runs out of the room, crying, and I feel proud of myself.

For the first time since Dad left us, I finally feel like him more than ever.

After I get cleaned up in the bathroom and dressed again, I make my way outside. I'm greeted by two angry men—a father and son glaring at me like I've committed some grave sin by making one of their own cry.

But that's just the thing they don't seem to understand. We're different, Cleo, Skylar, and I, and nothing will ever change that.

We grew up with Luke, whereas his rules were taken in and then regurgitated by Bryden to fit his own fucking needs, and that's no way to raise a family.

When I step out to join them, I notice that Xoe is still naked, shivering, and smells like a fresh fuck. I only hope that Skylar can't smell it too, but I don't think she can from where she's still playing with the kids.

She keeps casting odd glances in my direction, but I slide my hands into my pockets and shake my head. She doesn't need to know about what happened just yet. I'll tell her eventually, and then when she gets upset about it, I'll finally get her to admit that she *does* love me after all.

"What's going on?" I ask them as confidently as I can. I take a deep breath, clear my throat, then start again. And this time, I use a tone that would make Dad so fucking proud of me. "Is there a problem?"

Casey, seeing that I'm someone completely different

than who he first took me for, steals a glance at his father before he turns his body to face me. I can see the anger in his eyes and in the way he's chewing the inside of his mouth. I can also see the hurt he feels for his sister in the way he keeps clenching his fists, but it's gonna take a hell of a lot more than this to scare me.

If I want Cleo, I can't be Darby's son anymore.

I have to be Luke's.

"Casey," Bryden begins carefully. "Take your sister inside and get her cleaned up, okay? I need to talk to Richter."

He passes the blonde girl to his son who immediately embraces her, then stares daggers at me as he walks her back into the home and out of the snow.

"Think he'll fuck her next?" I ask with a smirk.

The words that escape me cause me to blink in shock rapidly, but I regain my bearings quickly. Dad would have said so much worse without a second thought and I have to... no, I *need* to be him.

It's time.

"You kids stay out here and keep playing," Bryden calls out to the gaggle of children before he gestures for me to follow him. Under Dad's rule, something like this meant time in the oubliette, but from what I've been able to gather in quick glances, Bryden doesn't have one.

Another way I know he's nothing like Luke. He has no way to punish his children if they step out of line, and they have to at some point because I refuse to believe that it's all a bed of roses here all of the goddamn time.

I follow Bryden into the living room where he motions for me to sit down in what I assume is his chair. It has to be because it's the biggest one and only kings own the mightiest of things—regardless of what they may be.

"Richter, I know that this is all a lot to grasp, but I assume that you can agree with me when I say this isn't how Luke raised you," he says as he sits down and rubs a hand tiredly over his face. "Regardless, you're in my house now, son. These are my rules, and I'd like you to respect them while you're here."

"Son?" I ask, a bite to my tone. "I thought you said I was your brother."

I see the infamous Greene rage flash in his eyes for a moment, but it's quickly replaced by a smile. It's almost like he knows how to control all of the things I've yet to learn.

"It's just how I address the children in this house, Richter," he finally says with a chuckle. The moment I open my mouth to tell him that I'm not a child, he quickly cuts me off. "Even though you hurt Xoe's feelings, I'd like to invite you and Skylar to stay with us tonight."

"No," I reply instantly but Bryden raises a hand. "It's dangerous outside with all of that snow coming down. What kind of man would I be if I knowingly let you both go out there and possibly get into a wreck that could have easily been prevented by giving you a place to stay for the evening? In the morning, if you're still feeling the same way you are now, you're free to go."

"I really don't think—"

"Skylar's already agreed," he continues. Almost as if I don't have a voice—as if I'm not sitting directly across from him. "She jumped at the chance to stay overnight with Cleo. I'm sure it would be easier for you three to bond again if you stayed here with us tonight. Cleo would understand it a little better if she goes to bed and sees you still here in the morning. The coming and going is what I think has her confused," he finishes thoughtfully.

I want to tell him to go fuck himself, but I can see the snow falling heavy through the windows.

"I won't take no for an answer, Richter," he exclaims in that annoying, cheerful tone of his as he gets to his feet. "Tonight, you'll both stay here, Skylar will help with the chores and getting the kids dressed and into bed, and you..." His voice trails off for a moment as his eyes lock onto mine. "You'll see what it's like to become a man in this house."

I don't want to stay—I don't, however, I never did get around to changing the tires on the truck and I could easily swerve if I hit a patch of ice hidden underneath the snow and it'd probably kill us both.

Maybe he isn't really worried about us dying so much as he is about us living differently than him.

That's fine.

If he wants me to become a man in *his* house, I'll show him what's it like to be *the* man in mine.

"Deal," I say, extending a hand to him and shaking it slowly.

And being a man in my house means following Luke Greene's fucking rules. Not his.

TWENTY-THREE

Bryden

I'm a patient man.

I know that some of my previous children might disagree with that, but I am.

I've always been patient. Ever since I used to have to sit silently in the bathroom while my whore of a mother banged random men in dingy hotels for a fistful of bills. And I developed my patience further at the bottom of the oubliette.

I bided my time before I showed Ella how to love me. I waited until each of my children were the right age, never rushing things unless they needed it. And if Richter thinks he can bait me into action before I'm ready... the boy is going to be gravely disappointed.

Not that I'm going to make him wait long.

He's been sulking and stomping around the house since our conversation. I can tell it's making Skylar nervous, but she doesn't have to worry. Everyone in my house is on alert now. They've seen his true colors.

I sit in my chair in the living room after dinner, listening to the girls explain the bedtime routine to Skylar. Heather shares some of her clothes with her and, just as I'd planned, Cleo is excited to have Skylar in her room for the night.

The little ones are already in their cribs, falling asleep amidst the sounds they've known since they were born. Everyone is doing what they're supposed to... and I'm waiting.

It doesn't take long for Richter to realize he doesn't have an assigned place to sleep, and after he's done harassing Skylar, he walks into the living room and drops himself onto the couch. Almost exactly where I taught Wesley how to receive my love.

"I guess I have to sleep out here?" he asks, pushing at the cushions, but I just raise a finger to my lips and point at the cribs.

"Come with me," I whisper. Standing, I move to the backdoor, opening it quietly. To my surprise, he follows me without any of his dramatic attitude. We both put our coats on in silence, and then I grab the flashlight and tuck it into my pocket before I step out onto the patio. In the open area of the backyard, the moon on the snow is more than enough light to see by. We won't need the flashlight until later.

Richter rubs his hands together in the chill, looking out over the landscape while I close the door, and then I move to stand beside him. Enjoying the silence, letting my patience test his—and I win.

"Okay, let's handle this," he says, turning to face me, and I chuckle as he shakes out his hands. If he thinks we're going to fight, he has no idea how different he is from our father.

Luke rarely went for the direct fight.

It was always so much easier to break the spirit first.

"I told you that if you wanted to be treated like a man in this house, I'd show you what that means."

"Just get it over with, Bryden," he snaps, trying to sound like he's in charge.

"I've already had the conversation with you that disrespect won't be tolerated in this house. Not to me, or to anyone in our family."

"You're not my family." Richter crosses his arms, staring at me, and I shrug, ignoring his comment.

"Tell me, did Luke allow disrespect in his house when you lived with him?" I ask, looking over at him, but I can read the quick flash of fear on his face. *No.*

"Dad never had to ask for respect."

"To be clear, I'm not asking," I reply, feeling the cold air fill my lungs on a deep inhale. "But when I was with Luke, he used to put us in the oubliette when we misbehaved. If we were disrespectful or disobedient or disappointing. Did he ever put you in the oubliette, Richter?"

"No," he answers, lifting his chin defiantly. "We knew how to behave when Dad told us to do something."

Right.

"Well, I feel it's only fair to let you know that my house has the same rules around disrespect, and I expect you to follow them."

"You're not my father," he growls.

"I'm well aware of who our father was," I answer with a chuckle, remembering the way Luke used to hit me in the back of the head when I made a mistake. How he'd do much worse when I was disrespectful or disappointing. It was harsh, but effective. "Wait here."

Richter watches me as I walk across the moon-drenched yard, stopping near the neat pile of logs Casey prepared for our family. Wrapping my fingers over the handle of the axe, I yank it out of the tree stump with a sharp tug. On my way back to the patio, I swing it onto my shoulder with a grin that feels natural, and Richter's eyes go wide.

He doesn't look like an angry young man anymore; he looks like a scared little boy.

"Look, Richter, I don't want to put you in the ground," I say, looking him in the eyes as I adjust the axe on my shoulder. "So, I'm giving you a choice."

"A choice?" Richter asks, trying to keep his voice steady, but he telegraphs his fear in the way he looks around. Searching for an escape, or someone that will help him... but he'll find neither.

"Yes. You can either choose to act like a man, or I can treat you like an errant little boy." The damn grin won't leave my face, and I can remember Luke holding a shovel just like this when he told me to bury Stephanie. It shouldn't feel right, I've always prided myself on my differences with Luke, but seeing the haze of panic on Richter's face is... satisfying. "What's your choice?"

"I'm not your son, or one of the little kids running around here. I have my own house, and I'm *the* man of my house."

"Okay then, I'm going to show you what it means to be *the* man of the house." Flicking the flashlight on, I point toward the tree line. "Go on."

"What?"

"Are you scared, Richter?" I ask, letting the grin stretch, and he shifts his eyes from me, looking at the dark woods.

"Fuck no," he snaps, straightening his shoulders as he starts to march across the snow. I keep the beam of the flashlight just ahead of his feet, keeping pace behind him, letting him slow when the denser snow at the base of the trees makes the path more difficult.

He glances back at me a few times, but once we're

under the trees I know he can't see a thing. All he can see is what the flashlight touches, occasionally getting glimpses of more when the moonlight peeks through.

We've been walking for about ten minutes when he pauses, and I shine the light into his face. Richter flinches, waving his hand at it, and I move it down to his chest so I can still see his angry expression. "Okay, Bryden, what are we doing out here?"

"Men's work," I answer, and he huffs.

"Bullshit."

So. Damn. Disrespectful.

"Richter... I know you never spent time down there," I begin, ignoring his comment as I flick off the flashlight so we're swathed in darkness. His breath hitches, and I smile as I continue. "But the oubliette is dark like this. When the lid is shut. Night or day... doesn't really matter. And right now, out here, you can at least smell the fresh air, the crispness. You can feel the open space around you even though you can't see it. Down there? This time of year, it's just cold. Bone-deep cold because the ground tries to leach the warmth out of you, and you can't stretch out because there isn't enough room. It's just you and the dark and the cold."

"He put you in there a lot?" he asks, but this time there's no superiority, no cocky tone.

"When I disappointed him." It's the only answer he's going to get. The boy thinks he was raised by Luke, but the man that raised me wouldn't have been so soft. I doubt he even had to thank Luke on his knees for dinner. Flicking on the flashlight again, I angle it ahead of us. "Let's keep going."

"Where?"

"I'll tell you when we get there, but you're just wasting

time." Looking up at the sky, I wait, showing him the power of patience once again, and eventually he mutters curses and continues on the path I light for him.

Another ten minutes pass, broken only by Richter cursing through harsher breaths, and I wonder if he's done any manual labor at all. *Did Luke never make him weed the yard on hands and knees? Haul logs across the yard? What's he been doing alone all these years?*

The thick trees finally break, and the moonlight is strong enough on the snow for Richter to see, so I turn the flashlight off to conserve the battery in the cold.

"What is this, Bryden?" he asks, and I can tell he's nervous.

"You're going to help us get a head start on that chicken coop Xoe wants."

"What! How?"

"You're going to chop down a couple of trees, cut the branches away, and separate them into more manageable logs." Swinging the axe off my shoulder, I hold it at my side and his eyes follow it. "Do you know how to chop down a tree, Richter?"

"You realize you can just buy wood, right?"

I chuckle, rolling the axe handle in my fingers. "We don't have the money for that, Richter. And why would I waste what I do have on *that* when there's plenty of wood right here?"

"You expect me to just chop down a tree?" he asks, a slight laugh in his voice, but it stops when I nod.

"I do. You want to be treated like a man, then you need to contribute like a man. Earn it." Pointing at the trees along one edge of the clearing, I show him where Casey and I have cleared trees in the past. "You'll want to stick to the edges. Look for a tree that the wind may have already angled toward the clearing, makes it easier to fell it the right direction."

"You're kidding right?" he asks, staring at me, and I let my grin stretch again.

"Want to change your choice, Richter?"

"No," he says quickly, turning back to the trees.

"All right then... listen up." I walk him along the tree line, using the flashlight sparingly to show him a few options, and then I explain the cuts. "Make the first notch on the side you want it to fall on, creating a triangle with a flat side on the bottom, and a cut-out at about a forty-five-degree angle. After that, switch to the opposite side of the tree, about a foot above your first cut, and you want to mimic the same cut. Alternate with flat and downswings. Got it?"

"I'll figure it out."

"Good," I reply with a smile. "Which tree do you want to start with?"

"I don't know. That one?" He points at one I'd suggested, and I walk over to it, hefting the axe.

"Hold it like this, and—" I pull it back and swing, embedding the axe head in the tree with a flat cut. Then I repeat with the downswing, carving out the first chunk of tree. "Just keep going until it's about a third of the way through on this side. I'll keep an eye on you."

Richter holds out his hand for the axe and I give it to him. There's a moment when he contemplates using it on me. I can see it in the side-glance, the shift of the axe head as he tests the weight of it, but I'm not concerned. If he wants to try it, he can, but I'll have to put him in the ground.

That will be too far even for my patience with my long-lost brother.

He lines up with the tree and swings the axe, scraping the tree when he doesn't land it fully.

"That's fine. Try again."

"I've got it!" Richter snaps, lining up again, and this time he hits the tree, the axe just doesn't go in very far.

I find one of the stumps, dust off the snow, and sit down to watch. He's aggressive at first, more concerned with looking tough than making any progress, but as the minutes tick by, he starts to get tired. He doesn't say anything though, refuses to show his weakness, and I respect that.

Luke never tolerated weakness anyway.

It takes Richter almost half an hour to get a third of the way through the trunk, and although the notch isn't quite big enough, I let it slide. "Go ahead and switch to the opposite side."

"God dammit!" Richter growls, resting the axe on the ground at his side as he breathes hard. "How long are you going to make me stay out here?"

"Until you're done."

"And when is that?" he snaps, and I want to drag him through the woods and show him what the strap feels like because I'm sure he's never felt the sting of it.

Luke was too gentle with him—something I wasn't sure was possible for the man. But *this* shitty attitude is why the rules matter. This is why my home has consequences, and the consistent use of them has meant I've had to implement them less and less. And Richter may not be mine, but that doesn't mean he gets to be disrespectful.

"Bryden!" he shouts, exasperation tainting his voice.

"I already told you what was required, Richter. Do you need me to repeat it?"

"Chop down trees," he mimics, lowering his voice a little in an effort to match mine. "How many fucking trees?"

"Two, but if you want to keep being disrespectful, I can make it three."

"You're not going to make it anything," Richter grumbles, dropping the axe into the snow as he walks away from me, but I don't bother moving. He gets to the trees and stops, unwilling to walk into the woods in the dark.

"Here's the thing, Richter. You don't know how to get out of here, and if you walk in the wrong direction... you'll be walking a very long time. In the cold." I point around us casually before resting my arms on my knees again. "Even if you're just slightly off, you won't find the house. A slight misstep here and two hundred feet later you're pretty off course, and there's not much out here."

"This is bullshit."

"This is a *consequence*, Richter," I say, grinning at him when he faces me again. "And, trust me, there are worse ones."

"If I chop down the two trees, you'll take me back?" he asks, digging in the snow for the axe.

"Then you're going to cut the branches off and cut the trees into smaller logs."

"That's going to take all night!" he shouts, kicking the tree in front of him.

"At this rate, I think you're right." Chuckling, I point at the tree. "May as well get started."

He hesitates, fuming in anger, but eventually he picks up the axe again and starts on the opposite side of the tree.

I wait for Richter to get into a rhythm with it, until he's no longer wasting energy on cursing or muttering about me. When his focus is completely on the task at hand, I stand up. "You're almost through a third up here. After that, switch back to your original notch. Keep alternating the swings but pay attention to the tree and figure out which way you're going to run when it starts to fall. Come up with a few paths before it falls."

"Okay," he says, bringing the axe back for another swing.

"Good. Since you're doing so well, I'm going to go get us some coffee and snacks to help us stay warm."

"You're going to leave me out here?" Richter asks, stepping away from the tree, and he definitely looks like a little boy right now.

"Not for long," I answer, walking toward the trees, and then I hear Luke's voice in my head, and I chuckle. "It's like our father used to say. Some time alone in the dark makes everyone rethink their choices."

"Bryden—"

"I'll be back soon, Richter. Just get that tree down and start stripping the branches off." I wave at him, flicking the flashlight on as I guide myself out of the woods. I've got things to check on in the house, but I won't leave him out there alone. Not *all* night. And I'll even bring back the coffee I promised.

Little things like that help to build trust.

Like food dropped into the oubliette.

By morning, Richter should have a better understanding of what it means to be a man and how one can never avoid consequences. And if his hands are blistered and bleeding—which wouldn't surprise me as unused to labor as they are—then those marks will help him remember that my rules aren't optional.

For anyone.

TWENTY-FOUR

Skylar

Cleo went back into her fort with Sierra after Heather left. Now it's just, me, the girls in their hideaway, and Moira. A gentle knock on the door greets my ears next, taking my attention away from my sister.

"What's the password?" Sierra shouts from inside the fort.

"Open sesame," comes the reply.

"You have solved the riddle, you may enter!" Cleo calls out, which sends both of the girls into a giggle fit. Moira goes over to stick her head into the fort, shushing them. "Everyone else is sleeping, you can keep playing as long as you use your inside voices, okay?"

One of the girls shoots their hands out and pulls Moira into the fort and I smile. They love her so much because they're used to her. It's no wonder no one here trusts me—they've only known me for the better part of a day.

Since the girls have become preoccupied with whatever game they're playing, I decide that I'll open the door and, hopefully, whoever is on the other side will provide some much-needed adult conversation. Something that doesn't have to do with rules, or how to do chores in a home I don't live in, or how to be a 'good child' to a man that isn't even my father.

Something... *normal*.

I put my hand on the doorknob and glance over my shoulder again before I pull the door open. When I do, I find myself staring into the same pair of eyes that led me into seduction not a few hours before.

"Hey." Casey greets me with a smile on his lips and a warmness to his gaze. "Is it okay if I come in?"

I want to tell him no, because it's not, but this isn't my room to shut him out of, so instead I nod and take a step to the side.

"Thanks," he says as he runs a hand back through his hair and walks into the room. I turn my face away from him when I notice his smile slipping into a grin, and he chuckles. "You can close the door if you want, Skylar. I'm just here to check up on my sisters and make sure that everything is okay before we go to bed."

"I'd rather not," I manage to squeak out. I'd hoped to sound more defiant than I do, but I can't seem to hold my ground against him for some reason.

Casey is just so much different than Richter in the way he treats me, and I think it's starting to have an effect on how I see my brother.

"Fine by me," he acquiesces with a shrug as he breezes by me and crouches down in front of the fort. "I know—no boys allowed—I'm not gonna come in. I was just wondering when everyone thought they'd be ready for bed?"

"Never!" comes the reply from whom I'm assuming are

Sierra and Cleo, and Casey shakes his head with a laugh as he gets back to his feet.

"Were you this difficult to get into bed?" he asks me with a smile.

"No. I listened when Mom told us it was bedtime," I respond with a shrug. It's the trust; there was never a moment that Mom asked us to do something that we disobeyed her. She never hit us, but the slightest misstep against either of the adults in the house would flip Dad's switch and he'd threaten to tan our hides.

After Mom heard his threat one time, she made us promise that we'd never talk back to either of them or tell them no to anything she asked. *Her*, not Dad—she wanted to keep us safe from what he was doing to her, which I later found out is exactly what Richter's doing to me.

"Can I ask you something?" I say to Casey nervously. He nods, moving over to where I'm still standing by the door, and holds a hand out to me. I stare at it uneasily before I take it and let him lead me to the bed.

"What's on your mind, Skylar?" he asks, the smile never faltering from his lips as we sit down.

"I... um..."

"You can talk to me, you know. I get that we don't know each other really, but family is family and I always take care of mine," he states in a gentler tone.

I take a deep breath and fold my hands in my lap. Staring at the top of them, I wonder if it's worth causing even more friction between our family and his, but I have to know the truth and the only way to get that is to ask.

"Does..." I bite my lower lip nervously.

"Does what?" he prods, resting a hand on top of mine.

"Does Bryden force you?" I ask, stealing a glance at him.

"Force me to what?" The confusion in his tone is

genuine and I can tell that beating around the bush isn't working with him.

"To... uh, love each other," I stammer out.

"No." His reply is instant, firm, and fierce. But not in the way that Richter would say something, and definitely not with the fierceness that Dad would speak down to Mom. "Our family is built on love—mutual love. We respect each other, know that we all deserve to feel happy, and being together the way we are is how we show it. Why? Has Richter forced you to love him?"

A change in the timbre of his voice sets me slightly on edge, but it's too late to turn back now.

"Sometimes," I confess, a tear rolling down my cheek and landing on the back of his hand.

A low growl escapes from somewhere deep within Casey as he turns to face me, bringing his hands up to either side of my face.

"Love should *never* be forced. It's something that you need to experience, that you both should be willing to give. I can show you how to love the right way if you'll let me."

I want to say no.

I want to get up and walk out of the still open door, but I don't. Instead, I go against my instinct, lean forward, and press my lips to his.

He smiles, a small breath escaping him, and I pull away. Maybe that was too forceful of me, maybe it's the exact opposite of what he wants to teach me, however, it's the first time that I've initiated a kiss with a boy, and I like the way it felt.

"I'm sorry," I tell him, feeling ashamed of my actions.

"For what?" he asks in a soft tone as he rests his forehead against mine. "I want you to love me, Skylar. You're not taking anything I'm not willing to give."

My breath shudders as Casey moves one of his hands away from my face, wrapping his arm around my waist to pull me closer.

"You have every right to claim what you want, you know. We're family, and this is how you'll know for sure that I'm not lying to you."

And there's that word again rearing its ugly head and trying to stop what suddenly feels so natural.

"Just follow my lead, okay?" he whispers before he lowers his lips to mine, brushing them gently. It sends a shiver through me, and for the first time it's not one of repulsion. It's hunger, need, and wanting the man that's before me instead of running away from him.

Casey lets go of me long enough to pull his shirt over his head and toss it to the floor, then he slips his hands under the edge of mine and does the same.

I reach for his pants, but he chuckles softly and pulls my hands away, kissing the tips of my fingers before looking into my eyes.

"Do you want to lead? Because I'll let you," he offers with a smile.

"No, that's okay," I reply quickly, shaking my head. Casey chuckles good-naturedly as he gets to his feet, reaching down for me to help me scoot toward the edge of the bed.

Using the tips of his fingers, he tilts my chin up, and as I look into those soulful eyes of his, I hear the sound of his zipper.

"Have you done this before?" he asks as he shifts slightly in front of me and I nod. I have with Richter, many times before, because he likes the way it feels.

And while I've never admitted it to him, sometimes I like the way it feels too.

"If anything makes you feel uncomfortable at any time, tell me and we'll stop, okay?" Casey says softly as he places a hand on my shoulder, bringing me a little closer to him.

Just by offering a reprieve, something that my brother has never done, I already know that I won't stop him. Casey is making this about both of us, not just him. That's not something Dad taught Richter to do.

In the bedroom is where you show her just how much the man of the house you are. You make damn sure she does what you say, when you say, and how you say it. If she fucks up, throw her into the oubliette for a few days and let her think about it. She'll do better next time, son.

As Casey gently presses the head of his hard cock against my lips, I decide that there's no way he's an actual Greene. He wouldn't allow me an escape route, nor would he be so caring with his *love*.

I let him part my lips, my eyes still trained on his, waiting for instruction like I would with Richter, but instead, a smile creases his lips as a shuddering breath escapes him—and he waits.

"It's okay, Skylar. I promise," he says with a nod, and that's when I begin.

I raise a hand, wrapping it around his shaft, and slowly start to move my head up and down his length. Casey's breath hitches when he moves his hand from my shoulder, resting it on the back of my head.

A soft moan escapes him as I begin to swirl my tongue around his flesh, continuing to bob my head, my hand trailing after my mouth's movements.

He groans slightly and I open my eyes to look up at him. I don't know if I'm messing this up, or hurting him, but when I see the way his eyes look—so hazed over with *love*, I continue.

A few more strokes of his cock with my tongue and hand and he lets out a chuckle, giving me the gentlest shove away.

"It's your turn now," he tells me, leaning down to pick me up and place me in the middle of the bed like I don't weigh a thing.

"My turn?" I ask in confusion as he begins to pull my pants down.

Casey stops for a moment, tilts his head to the side, then shakes his head, the smile still prominent on his handsome face as he reaches for my underwear next. Without another word spoken between us, he pulls them down and tosses them over the side of the bed, lying down with his head between my legs.

"Mm. You smell good," he murmurs, wrapping his hands around my thighs before he looks up at me. "Are you doing okay?"

I nod, still feeling a little confused at why he felt that I would get a 'turn.' When Richter goes down on me, it's always because he wants to and not because it's my 'turn.'

"Good," he replies quietly.

Instinctively, I reach up to grip the sheets above my head. I don't know how this is going to feel when someone else—

"Oh, God," I grunt as he begins to gently use the tip of his tongue to tease my clit.

This is so much different than Richter. Somehow, Casey knows exactly where my spot is, and he stays there, teasing me for a few more agonizing seconds before he slips his tongue into my core.

I grunt and let go of the sheets, reaching down for a fistful of his hair, and I do my best not to squeal, squawk, or scream.

None of it would be borne of forced intentions but, for the first time, honestly feeling completely fucking loved in a moment with someone.

Unlike someone I still haven't learned to love in the way he wants me to.

I should feel ashamed.

I'm betraying Richter again, but the only thing I feel as Casey begins to lap at me is the need for more.

"Does this feel good?" he asks after he pulls his mouth away and slips a finger into me.

"Yes," I manage to croak out.

He slides another finger into my wet opening and begins to move them in and out. His movements are gentle but commanding—he wants what Richter is always after, but the one thing my brother has to work so hard for is much easier for Casey to elicit from me.

He shifts on the bed again and begins to lick my clit, continuing the teasing thrusts with his fingers.

My eyes close tightly as the world around starts to become distant, hazy, and a little too far away. But I also know that the moment I come crashing back down to Earth, he'll be satisfied as long as I am.

I don't hear the door open nor the sudden silence in the room. The only thing I know is the moment I'm in; the only thing I hear is my own labored breathing, and the man that's causing all of it dutifully working for his reward.

A hand gently runs down the side of my face, followed by a familiar chuckle, but I keep my eyes closed.

This moment belongs to me and Casey and I don't want it spoiled by giving in to the temptation of seeing who's invaded our private moment.

A finger parts my lips on my next gasp and I begin to suckle on it. I want it to be Casey's, but I know it's not. He's much too busy fucking me with his fingers and holding me in place with his other hand.

And almost as quickly as I'm sucking the finger in my mouth, I'm not anymore.

The sound of a hand patting skin enters my ears next, then the footsteps retreat, followed by the door closing.

A loud moan escapes me as Casey tips me over the edge of this euphoric cliff that he's had me on the precipice of for what feels like forever... and it's over. Leaving a tingling hum behind in my veins.

He pulls his fingers out of me and moves to hover above me, a grin on his face. I place a hand against his cheek, a tired laugh escaping from me.

"Still okay?" he asks, brushing his lips against the palm of my hand, and I nod.

"See? Loving your family isn't the nightmare you were led to believe," he tells me with a smile.

A creak on the side of the bed draws my attention and I arch an eyebrow. Sierra is sitting next to where we're lying, watching us curiously, with Moira and Cleo standing behind her.

"Hey," Casey says to me. "It's just us."

His lips press hungrily against mine as he reaches down and presses his dick against my hole, then begins to gently slide inside me, drawing my attention away from the other young women in the room.

As Casey thrusts his hips, I dig my nails into the flesh of his arms. Something that's usually so mundane and unwanted shouldn't feel like this.

I arch my back slightly, ignoring the whispers next to us. Then the bed creaks again and Casey chuckles through a grunt.

"It's okay," he says. "We're all family and we love each other equally. Right, Skylar?'

I nod without opening my eyes again because I want him to keep loving me, so I'm willing to tell him anything he wants to fucking hear at this point.

One moment, my mouth is slightly agape and taking in ragged gasps of air, and in the next, warm, wet flesh is settled on top of it.

But instead of pushing away, instead of fighting, I reach up and use a hand to hold the newest component of our ecstasy in place. I know what to do. I know what feels good. So, I lick, finding her clit before I let my tongue slip into her wet hole and begin to fuck it as best as I can—the way Casey did with me.

She rocks her hips and begins to ride my tongue as Casey continues to fuck me. A little harder now, a little less gentle.

"More," she says in a strangled tone and I lean my face up as best as I can to go in a little deeper, switching to her clit when I can reach it.

She moves her hips faster. My face is getting coated with her juices, and while I've never done this before, I know now that this is how family *should* love each other... and that it's a choice and not a chore.

"You're both so fucking beautiful." Casey breathes as he slides out of me. "Up," he says, pulling her off me. "Skylar, turn on your belly. Sierra, go sit on the pillow."

I do as I'm told without hesitation and when Casey moves behind me and slides his cock into me again, Sierra grabs me by the hair and pulls me toward her pussy. I wrap my arms around her thighs and bury my face between her legs. She lets out a yelp as I do my best to continue licking and fucking her with my tongue while Casey watches us, thrusting his hips harder, going in deeper than before.

Another creak on the bed, and I feel a pair of hands as they pull me up to my knees. Casey digs his fingernails into my sweaty, slick skin as he chuckles.

The gentlest touch of fingertips grazes my belly, trailing down to settle on my clit, and I moan into Sierra's cunt. She grabs another fistful of my hair as she rolls her hips against me.

The finger on my clit begins moving in circles, sparking the rest of the senses I didn't even know I could feel right now.

"Can I?" asks a timid voice.

"Always," Casey grunts as he pulls me away from Sierra and holds me back against him. "Keep your eyes closed; it feels so much better when you only use your sense of touch," he whispers into my ear.

I nod as my breath hitches.

Casey groans into my ear, as the finger moves away from my clit, instead replaced by a tongue that's caressing his cock as it slides in and out of me.

Two hands, each belonging to someone different, grip my tits, and then begin to suck on my nipples. Gently, then roughly. Lovingly, then longingly as the members of Bryden's family show me what true love really is.

Casey's cock slips out of me for a moment, and as he holds me against him, I can hear hungry, sloppy sucking sounds.

"This is how we can be forever," he gasps into my ear. "Do you love me, Skylar?"

Before I can answer him, he thrusts back inside me, the finger returns to my clit, and my body begins to shake.

Teeth bear down around my nubs at the moment of my

climax and when it's finally over, when the finger leaves my clit, and my breasts are freed from the warm, wet restraint of hungry mouths, Casey pulls out of me and rests his chin on my shoulder as I shudder.

"Because I love you."

TWENTY-FIVE

Bryden

The sky is growing lighter, and I yawn, the strength of it cracking my jaw as I shake off the exhaustion. I'm tired, but I know Richter is completely wiped out. For the last couple of hours, every time he's brought the axe down on the tree it's taken him longer and longer to lift it again.

Still, there are two trees down. The branches have been piled to the side, waiting to become easy firewood once they're dry. And the first tree is already separated into manageable logs. Richter isn't quite halfway through the second tree, but with the growing light I can see the dark haze on the handle of the axe.

He's bled for this.

Worked hard to prove he's a man.

And I never expected him to finish the job in one night, although I would have been impressed if he had.

"You can stop." Standing, I stretch, feeling my joints arguing in the cold, but it's a good ache. A low burn in my muscles from sitting in the cold with him.

Richter doesn't reply as I pick up the empty thermos. The axe just hangs from his hand, the head of it buried in the snow, his arms limp at his sides. He's tired, and bleeding, and maybe now he'll actually listen to me. Maybe he'll accept the love this family could have for him like Skylar did last night.

She did so well.

For a moment I remember the way she was stretched out on Sierra's bed, so close to her bliss as Casey touched her. I couldn't resist touching her soft lips, sliding my finger into her mouth when she let out another sweet sound—and then she'd drawn me in. Sucked on my finger like she needed it.

I'd wanted to pull her to the edge of the bed and let her really taste me, show her how to express her love like I have with each of my children... but Richter was outside. Alone. In the dark. And although it was a punishment, I didn't want to leave him alone too long.

My self-control has always been my strength, and so I'd stepped back. Patted Casey on the shoulder so he knew I was proud of him without words, and then I waved to the rest of my girls. They always like to watch, to get involved, and I can only hope that they continued to show Skylar what is possible here. If she just accepts our love and joins us.

That thought pulls my gaze back to Richter who is still staring at the ground, breathing hard.

"You did well, Richter. Look at what you were able to accomplish with your hands." I gesture across the clearing. "All of this wood will be a part of a chicken coop in the spring, and you made that possible."

He still doesn't answer. He's not even looking at me, but that's okay. I know he has a lot to think about, and his body is beyond exhausted at this point.

"Let's get you inside. We'll warm you up, tend to your

hands, and let you rest before breakfast." Moving closer, I watch him carefully. The way his body sways a bit on his feet, the slight shiver as the sweat on his skin continues to cool. Reaching down, I take the axe from him and lift it onto my shoulder. "Come on."

Without waiting for a response, I start the walk back to the house. It's easier in the early dawn light, and as color returns to the world I can't ignore the stains on the handle of the axe. I left similar stains on the shovel that Luke made me use to bury Stephanie, and while it had hurt my heart at the time... I know it helped me be a better man.

Hard work shapes us, molds us, and while I meant this as a punishment, I think it will help Richter in the long run.

I'm sure it's something he won't forget.

A lesson from brother to brother.

A lesson our father never taught him.

We're almost back to the edge of the woods when I hear Richter's footsteps stop and I turn to look at him.

"We're almost there," I encourage, and he finally looks up at me.

"Bryden..." His gaze flicks over my face, and I turn toward him completely, sensing that there is something important happening inside him.

"Yes, Richter?"

"Did Dad have you do that? Chop down trees?" he asks, and I notice how his hands keep flexing. Probably so cold he can't feel the pain yet.

"No trees." Shaking my head, I glance toward the brightening pieces of sky through the trees. Hints of pink hitting the lower clouds as the sun pushes the darkness back. "Mostly yard work. Had to dig up a big rock from the yard and move it once. Took me a few days, and I wasn't allowed back in his house until I was done."

"Why did he make you do that? What did you do?"

"I didn't clean the kitchen right," I answer, catching the flicker of confusion on his face. "Luke told me that if I couldn't clean inside the house the right way, then I'd make the yard look better. So, he told me to move the rock and backfill the hole it left."

"Because you didn't clean the kitchen?" Richter asks, and I know that before last night it would have been doubt in his voice. Now… it's something else. I can tell he believes me. He just never saw that side of our father.

"Yes, because I didn't clean the kitchen well enough." I tilt my head in the direction of the house. "I know you're cold, Richter. Let's go inside."

He nods, falling into silence again, and I don't press him. Whatever he's thinking about is important, and I know that whatever he decides now will determine his fate.

Above ground with his family, or in the ground alone.

When we leave the shelter of the trees, he blinks at the sun on the horizon. It's all the brighter due to the snow, and I feel a little proud that he made it through the night to see the sun rise. There were a few moments I wondered if he would.

Like the time he spent alone out here.

He could have wandered off, got lost, or waited in the trees for me to return so he could come at me with the axe. I'd thought all of those things over while I made us a large thermos of coffee and packed a few snacks to keep his energy up. I'd planned how I'd handle him, no matter which choice he made… but when I got back to the clearing, he was already chopping branches off the tree he'd felled.

I think he felt pride in that moment too.

Seeing the results of his work laid out in the snow like

that, hefting the axe to continue it, *that* was the first time I think he's ever been a man—and I'm grateful I got to see it.

When I open the door to the house, I see him hesitate on the porch. He's looking inside, and I know he wants to go in, to warm up by the lingering heat of the coals in the fireplace, but he's just standing there.

"You're welcome in my home, Richter," I tell him, and he looks at me again. His eyes softer than Luke's ever were, and I know that has to be his mother in him.

"What do you want me to do?" he asks, and I smile.

Maybe the boy has learned a lesson.

"Come inside, warm up by the fireplace. I'll get the fire going again, and then we can get your hands cleaned up before you check on Skylar. And Cleo." Shrugging a shoulder, I lean my head toward the doorway again. "Come on, I know that you want to check on your sisters."

Richter nods, walking in ahead of me, and he fumbles with his coat and shoes, his fingers too cold and stiff to manage the small movements, but I don't try and help. I know he needs to do this himself.

A few minutes later I've got the fire stoked, flames licking at the fresh logs, and I pat his shoulder where he sits in front of it.

"You did well, Richter. I'm proud of you."

He looks up at me for a second, another odd look on his face, but I just smile.

"I'll get the first aid kit. You just stay here and get warm."

"And then I can see Cleo and Skylar?" he asks.

"Of course," I answer, my smile stretching into a grin as I head toward my room. "No reason to keep you apart."

TWENTY-SIX

Richter

The crackling warmth of the fire starts to beat on my cold, cracked skin.

When Bryden left me, I was afraid that it was going to be for the rest of the night. Dad would have without a second thought—he would have left me to die in the snow then had Skylar pick up the pieces of what was left of me to be discarded in the oubliette.

The threat was always there, lingering in the air like his bitter disgust when we would fuck up the most menial of tasks, though the only one of us to see the inside was Cleo. It's no wonder she cried when I threw the bread at her—it probably jogged that memory back and only God knows what was at the bottom of the fucking thing.

I rub my forearms, my teeth chattering as I try to speed up the process of warming my body. I close my eyes for a moment wondering if the Hell above ground is truly worse than what's down below in the oubliette, though I don't ever want to find out.

And with Dad gone, I know that I never will.

I open my eyes and glance up when I smell the fresh

scent of hot chocolate and nod at Bryden in thanks, taking the mug from his hand.

"Sip that slowly so you don't burn yourself," he says in a tone as tired as I feel. Though I honestly cannot imagine what's got him so fucking exhausted—he stood around watching while I chopped down his goddamn trees.

"I really appreciate the hard work you did out there, Richter. I almost felt like I was watching Casey chop the trees down. When I told you I was proud of you, I meant it. I know high praise isn't something you're probably used to, or ever got from Luke, but my word is my bond, son," Bryden tells me thoughtfully.

I raise the mug to my lips and swallow down the scalding liquid. Anything to take the pain of being called son away again. When I was a little boy, it was a title I held proudly. As a young man, the pride started to fade each and every time that Skylar cried in our bed when I would try to start a family with her, but it withered and died the moment I stepped foot into Bryden's home and saw just how different his family works from how ours did.

"I'm not your son," I mumble under my breath.

"What's that?" he asks with a chuckle.

"Nothing."

I decide not to press him. It wasn't meant for him to hear anyway but saying it out loud helps me feel like more of the man I was before I found this place, than the boy he continues to treat me as.

"Once you've finished your drink and have warmed up, you can go check on the girls," he tells me as he rubs his face tiredly.

"Can't I just take this into the room?" I inquire curiously.

"You can, sure, but I think it would be best if you give

yourself a chance to catch your breath before you go in is all."

I hate the logical way he thinks, but he's right. If I go in there shivering and looking like I've been awake all night, Skylar will be worried, and Cleo will more than likely be even more afraid of me than she already is.

"Good morning, Daddy."

I glance toward the doorway and see Xoe standing there, hands clasped in front of her, eyes on the floor and looking a bit subdued. She looks nothing like the girl I first met, and, in a way, I feel proud knowing that I have something to do with her current demeanor.

A smirk curves the edge of my mouth as I set the mug down on the floor and turn my body away from the door. I lean forward slightly and begin to rub my hands in front of the fire. If she thinks that her pouting and sulking will make me feel bad after the night I've had, then she's got another thing coming.

"Good morning, Xoe," Bryden says as cheerfully as he can. *Even the Stepfords have their limits, I guess.*

"Would you like anything in particular for breakfast?" Xoe asks in a hushed tone and I roll my eyes. After the years I spent alone with Skylar's fucking attitude, moping isn't going to work on me.

"Richter?" Bryden asks.

I glance over my shoulder and see his eyes on me expectantly. He's giving me the choice and I know it's only because he sees me as a man now, but I just shrug and shake my head before I turn my attention back to the fire.

"Anything you're up for making it seems," Bryden tells Xoe with a chuckle.

"Do you want me to check on Sierra and Cleo too, Daddy?" she asks before she leaves the room.

"That's alright, sweetheart. Richter will go check on them shortly."

"Good morning," she calls out to me softly. I let my eyes wander over to her for a moment, hold the gaze I can tell is painful for her to keep, then nod before turning back to the fire.

I've had enough of this bullshit.

I pick up the mug, shoot back what's left of the hot brew, then get to my feet doing my best to ignore the scalding feeling inside my throat. "How do I get to my sisters?"

Bryden rubs the bridge of his nose and I can almost swear he's hiding a smile on his face at the same time, but when he drops his hand and lets out a heavy sigh, I wonder if I'm just seeing shit.

Lack of sleep will probably do that to a person whereas exhaustion most definitely will. And it just so happens that I'm on both ends of that spectrum and I want my own fucking bed in my own fucking home with *both* of my sisters.

"Which way to Skylar and Cleo?" I ask Bryden evenly.

He gets to his feet and shakes his head. I think he can tell that the lesson he tried to teach me has fallen away like the trees I chopped down, but the difference is that he can't make an inferno out of fires that I refuse to light. Unlike him, I wouldn't piss on him if he were on fire, and I sure as hell wouldn't start one for him if he were as close to freezing to death as I was.

"Are you sure that you don't want to take a little longer to relax?" he asks with that smile of his.

I shake my head vehemently. "I'd like to see them now."

"Alright, follow me then," he says as he leads the way out of the room and into the hallway.

I'm still gripping the mug tightly in my hand, and while its empty now, it provides me comfort in an odd way. It also gives me the idea to crack the fucking thing across the back of Bryden's head, grab my sisters, and run the moment we get to them, but I know I won't have the strength to pull off such a daring plan right now.

I look down at my hands when the searing pain of the hot mug finally starts to set in. Now that I'm warming up and my nerves are coming back to life, I can feel pain again and truly understand the shit he just put me through.

They feel as raw as they look, the blood is almost completely dried on the cuts I received when splintering the trees just the way he wanted them. I know that the smallest misstep will more than likely break the scabs and cause the cuts to bleed again but I can't focus on that now.

I have my sisters to save.

A house of my own to get back in order.

And none of this has to do with Bryden or his family.

A renewed determination starts to course through my veins and I begin to chew on the inside of my mouth to ignore the now searing pain in my hands.

Bryden stops at a door by the bathroom, raises his fist, and knocks gently as I move the mug from one hand to the other.

Maybe if I divide the pain evenly, it won't hurt so much when—

"Richter?"

The shriek draws my attention away from my hands as I glance up and almost instantly black out from the rage rising within me.

What greets me when I look into the room is a betrayal that I never knew I would have to face.

Not from my own fucking wife.

"What the fuck are you doing?" I shout at Skylar, the mug dropping from my hand and shattering on the floor.

She tries to push Casey away, who's now looking at me with a smile on his face while my fucking wife straddles him like it's the most natural thing in the world.

He leans up and gives her a gentle squeeze before he lifts her up and lets her slide off the bed. Skylar grabs for one of the sweaty, betrayal-stained sheets to cover herself and immediately begins to cry.

In shame?

Was she forced?

I don't know and I don't fucking care. She's not his to touch.

And as suddenly as the rage sweeps over me, the calmness settles. I take a deep breath, walk into the room paying no mind to the three young women now huddled in the corner and extend my hand down toward Skylar.

Her sobs are falling on deaf ears as Casey watches us carefully. If he makes a move to stop me, I'll find the strength to throw him out the window.

Skylar finally takes my hand and gets shakily to her feet, sobbing her apology over and over, but I don't hear it.

I don't hear much of anything other than the beating of my heart in my ears and that's more than enough for me.

I yank her close to me, look into her shame-filled eyes and mutter a simple command. "Get your fucking clothes on."

She moves as quickly as she can, the sin that Casey tried to implant in her sliding down her thigh and I crack my neck.

When I look into the corner of the room and let my eyes focus, I see Cleo—naked, crying, and afraid.

A small smile curves the edge of my lips as I walk over to where she's standing and hold a hand out to her.

"There's nothing to be afraid of, little sister. I'll protect you just like I always did," I tell her in a soft tone I don't recognize.

But she does.

I can see it in her eyes, and as she throws herself into my arms and I hold her close, I turn my eyes toward Bryden who's watching the entire scene unfold with a cautious look on his face.

"We're going home now, Cleo. You, me, and Skylar. Together—just like Dad would want us to be."

TWENTY-SEVEN

Bryden
___

Watching Cleo, *my* Cleo, hugging Richter after his little outburst has my blood pressure rising. I really thought he'd learned his lesson, or at least *a* lesson, last night... but it seems he hasn't.

Disappointing.

The room is chaotic, and it's not the normal chaos of my home. No, this is anger and sadness and panic—and it's getting under my skin.

Richter is mumbling something, telling Cleo more bullshit lies, and everyone is too loud. I fucking hate hearing the girls cry. It grates my nerves. Cleo's is quieter, muffled against Richter's shirt, but Skylar's is loud, hiccupping, and so clearly filled with terror that I know exactly what she expects to happen if I let him take her.

Worse, Sierra won't stop whining.

"Cleo! You can't go!" Sierra shouts, her voice an irritating keen. Starting to cry herself, she tugs at her sister's arm. "Please, Cleo!"

"Daddy—" Casey starts to speak, but I raise a hand and

he stops. Sierra goes quiet too, looking at me desperately, and I take a slow breath.

Stay calm. No one has left yet.

"Why don't you speak up, Richter?" Watching him, I can't help but feel a smile spread over my lips because he nudges Cleo behind him with a hand on her rounded belly. She's mine whether he thinks so or not. She carries my child, and that's something he can't deny.

"We're leaving."

"You are?" I ask, laughing a little as I rub my hand over the scruff on my chin.

"What's so funny?" Richter snaps.

"I can see that Cleo remembers you and Skylar, and I'm relieved that you've reconnected... but if you think I'm going to let you take them home in an unsafe vehicle"—I shrug, spreading my arms a little—"I'm afraid you're confused."

"You can't keep her here. Cleo *wants* to come home with me," he argues.

"I can see that, and as always I want all of my children to be happy, but—"

"She's not your child! She's not yours at all! You're not her *Daddy*. She had a dad, *my* dad, and you're not him. I don't give a fuck who raised you, or how we're related, she belongs with me!"

Maintaining the smile isn't as hard as I thought it would be. The rage is simmering down deep, keeping my head clear, letting me think through my options, and even though the simplest solution would be to slit his throat and throw his traitorous body out the back door into the snow... it wouldn't bring me the results I want.

"What do you mean he's not my Daddy?" Cleo asks, and Richter smiles as he turns to talk to her, but I speak first.

"No matter what, Cleo is carrying my child, and I care about all of you being safe on the drive home."

"You're going to let them come with me?" he asks, and I can see the disbelief on his face.

"Daddy, no!" Sierra whines, tears rolling down her cheeks. "He can't take Cleo! He—"

"Be quiet, Sierra," I command, and she shuts her mouth like a good girl, even though she's still sniffling loudly. Looking back at Richter, I smile again. "Family needs to be with family, and I'm happy to help make that happen. However, we're going to need to take care of your tires before you go."

"The tires will be fine," he replies through clenched teeth, but I just laugh a little, shaking my head.

"No, they won't, and you know it too. You really want to put your sisters in jeopardy? You want to risk Cleo losing her baby because you dislike me so much?" The questions hover in the air, and I can see him turning over his options, trying to figure out a way out of this, but I know I haven't left him one. "It's barely dawn, Richter. Let the girls shower, eat some breakfast, and Cleo will be all packed up before we get back."

"Get back from where?" he asks, glaring at me with all the hate I know he feels for me.

"Town," I answer, pushing off the exhaustion I feel, because this is much more important. "I'm friends with one of the mechanics and I know he'll give us a good deal on some new tires. Won't take long at all."

"I'm not leaving them here," Richter growls, but I laugh again.

"And what do you think is going to happen to them?" I ask, grinning when his face flushes with anger, his glare turning on Skylar as she buttons her jeans.

"Think you can keep your legs closed while I get the tires, Skylar?" Every word is dipped in venom, and her eyes go wide as she nods at him.

"I'm sorry, Richter. I am. I'm s-so sorry," she babbles, but he lets out a sound of disgust as he turns back to me.

"When we get back, I'm leaving with *both* my sisters. Got it?" Richter stares me down, and I can tell the smile I'm holding is bothering him.

"Absolutely." Gesturing to Casey, I tilt my head toward the door. "Casey, come talk to me real quick. You'll be in charge while we're gone."

"Mind if I drive?" I call out, watching Richter as he speaks to Skylar. Based on the look on her face, and his hold on her arm, I can imagine he's threatening her, but that stops when he turns to look at me.

"No one drives the truck except me," he calls back, and I chuckle, leaning against the driver's side of the truck.

"You've got bad tires, don't know where we're going, and don't know the roads to get there." Shrugging, I point in the direction of town. "It's a pretty long drive, Richter, and I know where the ice likes to build up. We'll get there faster, and safer, if I drive."

Skylar says something to her brother, and he rounds on her, but I can't hear what he says—I just hate how he's touching her. It's not loving. Not kind. It's cruel, possessive, and unwarranted.

"Of course, if you insist on driving and wreck your truck, you'll be stuck here with us longer than you'd like." I smile, tilting my face up toward the sun. "But, as I keep saying, you're all welcome to stay here as long as you like."

"Fuck that," Richter growls, stomping toward me, but I don't turn my gaze to him until he stops a few feet away. He's holding his keys out toward me, and I take them with a wide grin.

"Good choice."

"You're only driving because the idea of my sisters being trapped here one more fucking day is worse than letting you drive *my* truck."

"Noted," I reply, pushing off the truck to open the driver's side door. Waving goodbye to Casey on the porch, I know I don't have to worry about anything. He'll do exactly as I asked.

He's always been a good boy.

TWENTY-EIGHT

Skylar

I'm standing on the porch watching Bryden turn the truck around as Richter watches me with stony eyes from the passenger seat. He never lets anyone drive that damn truck besides him, but I know he couldn't argue with Bryden's logic no matter how angry he still is.

I sigh when the truck moves slowly out of sight, wondering if Richter will ever come back for me again, but the thought is torn away from me by the young man that stayed behind with the rest of us.

Casey comes over and rests a hand on my forearm. "You should probably get showered up before they get back," he tells me softly.

"Yeah," I agree with a nod as I wipe a tear away from my face. The taste of Sierra lingers on my lips and the feeling of Casey's seed on my inner thighs makes me realize that there's more than just the physical body that needs to be cleaned.

I have to find a way to purge myself of the atrocities I've committed in the name of a love I haven't earned nor deserve.

Dad always had one simple rule when it came to whoever shared his bed and that was to never betray his heart. While sometimes I honestly don't think he had one, I realize now that it's more than likely what drove him to be the man he was.

Our grandmother betrayed him—she must have, even if we never knew how. Mom's betrayal came the day she tried to push him into the oubliette, though we never got the exact story. I know that he must have embellished it to suit his own agenda because I never do recall Mom being a mean or angry person.

Only when she was trying to protect us from Dad, I think sullenly as I finally turn on my heel and walk into the house. Casey follows, but not too closely—I know he doesn't understand the damage he's caused to my family because this is how he was raised, but I know it's irreparable in Richter's eyes and I can't fault him for it.

Luke Greene was a man with his own rules that were set forth in stone and etched in fire.

I've broken one of his cardinal sins by bedding a man that wasn't his son, and I know that I'll have to atone for that one day soon.

"Come on," a small voice says to me. I glance up and see Xoe holding a hand out toward me.

If I betrayed Richter, then he betrayed me too and *his* sin is standing in front of me.

I don't know exactly what—if anything—happened between the two of them, but she's a jezebel ready to tempt him away from me at a moment's notice.

Maybe I should let her, I think as I shake my head at her hand. She shrugs and leads the way to the bathroom where Moira has already laid out clean clothes and underwear for me. As I close the door behind me to have some privacy, it makes me wonder how many times this could have happened before to make everyone seem so goddamn prepared for the fallout that was bound to happen.

I lean into the shower and turn the knobs, holding a hand under the torrent of water until I find a temperature I'm comfortable with, then remove my clothes. I can't look at my reflection in the mirror even though it's right beside me because the girl that will look back at me isn't the same one that I was yesterday or the day before that.

I'm not ready to come to terms with the new Skylar until I've had the chance to talk this out with Richter. I'll apologize more sincerely than I ever have, and he'll forgive me.

He has to.

We're family.

"Looks like you're feeling better, Skylar," Xoe says politely when I join her and Casey in the kitchen.

"Mm," I grumble without meeting his eyes. He's trying desperately to catch mine, but I think I've given him more than enough at this point.

"How long do you think they'll be gone?" I ask her quietly.

"With the weather outside and those bum tires on the truck, who knows," she answers with a shrug. "Are you hungry, though? I made breakfast."

"I'm not hungry," I reply quietly.

"You have to eat something," Casey pipes up as he walks over to stand next to Xoe. "Fix her a plate and I'll see if I can get her to eat before we start moving things around."

I arch an eyebrow curiously at Xoe, though my thoughts

are toward what Casey said. Move what around? And why can't he wait until Richter gets back?

Questions asked out of place is what got Grandma thrown into the oubliette. Not doing as you're told to do is why Mom went down there eventually, too.

But there are no oubliettes on this property, so I know I can hold my ground against eating if I want to.

That is until Cleo walks into the kitchen and wraps her arms around me, resting her chin on my shoulder. She's fresh from the shower too and her round belly presses hard into my side.

"Hey, Cleo," I say to her softly.

"Hi, Skylar," she replies in a shaky voice.

I gently wrestle an arm out of her embrace and wrap it around her swollen waist, holding her close as I sigh.

"Are you hungry?" I ask, and she nods.

"Two plates, please," I tell Xoe as I lead Cleo to the table and sit down with her. My little sister never did like to eat alone. She was always afraid that it meant she was taking more of her share than she should and with the fear of Luke Greene always hanging over our heads even now, I understand her plight.

"Mind if I join you?" Xoe asks politely.

I shrug and pull Cleo's chair a little closer to mine, push her hair out of her face, and smile at her when she gives me a timid look.

"It's going to be okay; I promise. Once Richter gets back, we're going home," I tell her softly.

Cleo perks up slightly and I clear my throat to keep from crying. I don't know what Richter told her when they talked, but she finally understands that this isn't her home and isn't fighting the prospect of leaving with us.

Why the sudden change in her stance doesn't bother me more is something I choose to ignore.

Cleo won't be going back to the Greene Family Hellhole—not if I can help it.

Xoe comes over to the table a few minutes later and sets a plate down in front of my sister, then one for me, before she retrieves her own.

I hear the front door open and close a few times while we're sitting, eating our meals in silence. Other people are waking up in the house, moving around, I can hear water running in the pipes, and so I don't look to see who it is. Because even though I don't know a lot about how the outside world works, I know that Richter and Bryden couldn't have returned already.

I watched him change the tires on his beloved truck once and it took him at least half an hour to get one of them done, let alone having to drive into town to replace four.

Twenty minutes later, we're done with our breakfast and Xoe is busy making more plates for the others that have drifted in. We both thank her for the meals even though I want to smash my plate into her face.

Something about her irks me.

Maybe it's the way she trots around the house like a trollop, or maybe it's the way she turns up the dial on the meter when Richter is around, I'm not entirely sure.

Either way, I know she's not my friend. No matter how many different faces she can wear in one day.

"Okay, are we ready?" Casey asks as he enters the kitchen and rubs his hands together.

"For what?" I inquire, finally looking at him.

"I'm going to take you and Cleo home," he reveals with a big smile. "I figure why wait until they get back, you know? We can bring Sierra along so the girls are happy, and this way Cleo can start getting used to your place again as soon as possible."

My brow furrows in confusion and Casey laughs lightly.

"I'm just trying to help, Skylar, but if you'd rather wait until Dad and Richter get back, we can do that too."

I get to my feet and help Cleo get to hers. Wrapping an arm protectively around my little sister's shoulders, I shake my head.

"We'd like to go home now."

Casey's grin widens and even Xoe lets out a chuckle by the stove where she's still busy.

"Then let's go," Casey says happily. "Once we get on the road, you can tell me how to get home."

TWENTY-NINE

Bryden

"What the fuck is going on, Bryden? We've been gone for hours already." Richter paces across the small waiting room of the repair shop once more, rubbing a hand over his hair as he glances out the small window in the door for the hundredth time.

"Bill has the right tires now and he's putting them on. We'll be back on the road in no time," I answer, smiling at him as I sip another cup of coffee. It's bitter, nowhere near as good as the way Xoe makes it, but I keep drinking it to stay sharp.

"You said this wouldn't take long," he grumbles, pacing across the room again.

"My family lives in the middle of nowhere, Richter. Just getting to town took an hour, and Bill opened early for us when I called him. Honestly, this is going pretty quickly." I check the clock on the wall, unable to suppress my grin because I'm well aware of what's happening back home. "It's not even eleven yet. You should sit down, have some coffee, or water."

"This is bullshit," Richter mutters, but he stops at the

little table to make himself a coffee. He fills it with several plastic containers of creamer and more sugar packets than I can stomach to watch, but he finally sits down in the farthest chair from me.

"I hope you know that I truly am glad Cleo has remembered you. She deserves to have her entire family."

"You're *not* her family." Leaning forward, Richter braces his elbows on his knees, holding the coffee between his legs as he stares holes in the floor. His anger radiates off him in waves, but that's just because he hasn't learned to control it yet. I've acted brash in the past, but I've learned it's better to stay in control. Easier to be calm, controlled... especially when hard decisions must be made.

"You're my brother, and therefore she's my sister. Just like Jocelyn."

"Jocelyn?" Richter repeats, looking up at me with his brows furrowed, and realization slowly dawns on me.

"What was your mother's name, Richter?"

"Darby." His tone is cautious, but his curiosity has drained the anger from him, which is good.

Shaking my head, I chuckle a little under my breath. "Luke got farther than I thought it seems."

"What do you mean? Who's Jocelyn?" Richter sits up, focused on me now and not the extended time Bill has taken on the tires per my request.

"Jocelyn was my sister. She was born when I lived with Luke, and after that he sent me away because his new wife didn't like me." I shrug, relieved those old wounds don't sting the way they used to. "If I had to guess, I'd bet Jocelyn was Darby's mother."

"My grandmother?" he asks, but it's not directed at me. He's just processing the information, rolling it around in his head, so I stay quiet. Sip my coffee, watch the second hand of the clock tick more time away, waiting for him to speak again. "Did... did Dad have any other kids?"

"I don't know. I was his first born, but he didn't know about me until I was seven. There weren't any other kids until Jocelyn was born the year I turned fifteen." Glancing toward the door, I take a slow breath remembering how much I'd begged to stay when Luke kicked me out.

I didn't want to go back to my mother. Whore, drug addict... it had felt like a death sentence. Worse than the oubliette could ever be, but it had led me to Marian. Brought me my family, and in some ways I think Luke must have known I would carry on his legacy.

I'm sure it's why he came to find me, to see what I'd done with my family. He took Tristan and Xoe to bed when he visited, and there's a chance one or two of the kids could be his—which would only mean our family is closer than Richter could ever imagine.

But all of that is too much to press on the boy right now. I know if he has any hope of saving himself, I can't tip the scales with knowledge that doesn't matter anymore.

All that matters now is the family still above ground. The ones who can carry on the Greene Family legacy.

"I never knew her name," he mumbles, taking another sip of his coffee as he stares at nothing.

"Then I'm glad I was able to give you that. I wish I knew more, Richter."

"Well, like you said. You weren't there. Dad didn't *want* you, and I don't either." Standing up, he glances out the door again before muttering a curse under his breath. "I'm going to the restroom. Tell your friend to hurry up."

"Sure," I reply, smiling at him as he stomps into the small bathroom behind the counter and shuts the door too hard.

Rising from the chair, I dig in my pocket for the little pill I brought from home. There's still a few more leftover from when Damon broke his arm falling off the damn roof, and I know it'll help Richter give into his exhaustion on the drive to our home.

Moving quickly, I set it on the table beside his coffee and take out my pocketknife. I cut it in half, then cut those pieces in half, and use the flat of the blade to crush them into as much of a powder as I can. With all the sugar Richter dumped in his coffee, he likely won't notice the taste, but he only needs a bit anyway. Brushing the powder into my hand, I put it in his coffee, swirling the cup a few times before I dust off the table and return to my seat, grabbing a magazine to flip through it.

When the bathroom door opens a couple of minutes later, Bill is already walking inside, giving me a nod. "About done, just need to know how you're paying before I take the truck down."

"I've got it," Richter says, and Bill glances at him for a second, but then his eyes are back on me. He waits until I nod, acknowledging he's stalled long enough, before he walks over to take Richter's money.

The town we live near is small, mostly farmers and their families, and the best part of it is that everyone minds their own business—but they protect their own. And whether Richter realizes it or not, he's an outsider here.

"Took long enough," Richter snaps as he pays, and I put the magazine aside to stand up.

"That wasn't polite," I chastise, my voice carrying more of an edge than I want it to, but disrespect pisses me off almost as much as betrayal. "You should apologize to Bill. He's helping us out and he gave you a good deal on the tires."

"Sorry," Richter says insincerely, glancing at Bill who just stands behind the register with his arms crossed. The man doesn't move, or reply, and Richter groans. "Look, I appreciate your help, I just need to get home to my sisters. I'm sorry, okay?"

"All right," Bill replies, nodding his head once before he moves toward the door. "Just a few more minutes and you'll be ready to go."

"Thanks," Richter says, and I smile at Bill when he pauses at the door to look at me.

"Yes, thank you very much, Bill. You're always such a help." I wait until the door shuts again before I grab my coffee and take a long drink. "You might want to finish that coffee if you want to last the day, Richter. Neither of us got any sleep."

"And whose fault was that?" he snaps, but he grabs his coffee anyway, tossing back a swallow as I chuckle.

"I think we both know whose behavior led to us spending the night in the woods."

"You're an asshole," Richter growls, moving to the door to watch Bill out the small window, but he keeps drinking the coffee as I ignore his little outburst. A minute later he turns to look at me. "No comment about my language?"

"You know how you're behaving, Richter. Do you really need me to point it out to you?" I ask, holding the smile on my face as he grumbles and finishes his coffee, tossing the cup in the trash can with more force than necessary.

"You're just pissed off that Cleo knows you're not her *Daddy*." Richter laughs, a harsh, cruel sound. "She's not happy that you lied."

"She's a simple girl, Richter. Would you have rather I told her that her father didn't want her? That he dumped her in my arms when she was only five years old, crying and wailing and calling out to him while he walked away?" I spread my arms. "All I did was welcome her into my family and raise her as my own. She called me Daddy because her brothers and sisters called me that. I never made her do anything."

"So she *wanted* to be in your bed?" Richter asks, and I sigh, not wanting to have this discussion with Bill so nearby, but I know he won't drop it.

"Of course she did, Richter. Cleo wanted a baby. She wanted to be a mama like her sisters, and so I gave her that. Would you have rather I treated her differently her entire life? Alienated her? Left her unloved, lonely?"

"No," he grumbles, turning away from me. "She should have been with us."

"Luke thought differently," I answer, and the door opens, Bill holding it in one hand as he waves toward the truck.

"Thanks for the business, Bryden," he says, shaking my hand as I walk out after Richter.

"You are the best." Smiling at him, I accept the keys and shade my eyes against the winter sun. "Not sure the next time Casey and I might come by for parts, but we'll see you then."

"See you then. Drive safe," Bill replies, walking inside, and I shake my head as I see Richter standing by the driver's side of the truck.

Heading toward him, I tuck the keys into my pocket just as a yawn cracks his jaw. "I'll drive us back."

"They're new tires, Bryden, I can—"

"You still don't know the way, and you're exhausted. Just let me drive us home, you can rest, and that way you'll be ready to drive the girls."

Richter rubs the heel of one hand into his eye, a quiet

groan leaving him before he finally relents. "Fine. You can drive back."

I'm pretty sure he calls me an asshole again as he walks around the truck, but I don't care. He'll be out as soon as we leave Main Street.

Two and a half hours into the drive, Richter is sound asleep against the window. He's snoring lightly, and I'm not surprised that in sleep he reminds me a little of my sons. It's something about the way his face softens when all of that righteous anger fades away.

I can see a little of Wesley, Damon, and Casey in him—and I'm sure I see a bit of myself too. All remnants of Luke Greene. His cheekbones, his strong jaw, his hairline, the overall shape of his face... he's inside both of us. All of us.

For a minute I let the rush of sorrow run through me. He was my father, he shaped me into the man I've become through his actions and his choices, and he's gone. I never got to tell him goodbye. Not *really*.

That last 'bye' on the front porch of my house wasn't enough. I was so preoccupied with Cleo in my arms that I don't think I even watched him drive away. The last time I ever got to see my father, the man who gave me life... and I didn't even wave.

Glancing over at Richter again I acknowledge that I feel some jealousy. Similar to how I resented Jocelyn for so many years—but I doubt I'll ever find out what happened to her, or Richter's mother. Betrayal isn't something Luke tolerated, and I'm the same way. While I didn't agree with all of his methods, I learned quickly that when you want to keep a family together, sometimes you have to take action.

Sometimes you have to do the hard thing so that everyone else can be happy.

I don't ask for much. Respect, loyalty, love. Those things shouldn't be difficult in a family, they should be natural, but Luke must have been too old when Richter was born to pass on those first lessons.

The boy and his sister were on their own for too long. Abandoned, unloved, without anyone to guide them or give them direction, and I've tried to offer that.

But I don't think anything I do will be enough for Richter.

This will be his last chance. His last opportunity to show me he wants to be a man in this family. If he accepts the incredibly gracious opportunity I've set in front of him... then we can work this out. We can unite Luke's legacies into one family. One home.

This home.

Pulling into the driveway sends a buzz down my spine. It's been decades since I saw this house, but it hasn't changed much. It looks older, more worn, but so do I.

Glancing into the rearview mirror, I see Luke's eyes staring back at me. The creases at the corners formed from years of smiles, the scruff on my cheeks that reminds me so much of him.

Of what I owe to him. To his name.

To the legacy of the Greene family.

And I always swore to him that I'd be the perfect son, no matter what.

THIRTY

Richter

I grunt and shift as the earth continues to move beneath me, but this is different.

It's not the smooth sensation of tires over gravel, or even the slow travelling over the crunching snow to make it back to Bryden's home. It's almost as if I'm weightless right now... but still moving somehow.

I guess I was a hell of a lot more tired than I thought because I passed out almost as soon as I got into the passenger's side of my truck for the ride back. The last thing I remember was Bryden telling me to rest easy, that we'd be home soon, then the feeling of the truck slowly pulling out into traffic.

And almost as quickly as the new sensation begins, it's gone. There are a few low murmurs coupled with the stillness and feeling of comfort as my body rests on something, but I pay it no mind.

I turn over on my side, curl up into a ball, and surrender myself to the serenity of sleep again.

"Fuck," I grumble as the pounding ache in my head jolts me awake. I reach up and rub my eyes with the back of my hand, letting out a tired yawn.

Being awake all night is obviously not something I was built for, but manual labor has never been a big part of my life.

Dad would do most of the heavy lifting until he got sick, then I figured out a way to do things without becoming physically exhausted. Granted, I've broken a sweat here and there, mostly to impress Skylar and show her what kind of man she has, though I've always stopped before feeling like I overexerted myself.

Someone should tell Bryden that not everyone is built to fucking chop trees down, I think irritably as I smack my lips together.

I let out a sigh as I open my eyes, then smile when I see the back of the couch. *My* couch, not Bryden's. It's nice to be in a home where I have control and there aren't any weird rules about fucking everything that moves.

I sit up and rub my eyes again, then scratch the back of my head before I get to my feet. Of course, the entire thing could have just been a goddamn nightmare. I'd been having a lot of those since Dad died, though I never told Skylar.

I don't ever want her to see me as weak, but I've been thinking about Dad a lot lately, trying to figure out where my faults in being a man lie. I know I have them, so many that it's to the point where the woman that's meant to be my wife doesn't even enjoy my company in our bedroom.

I shake my head.

'She'll learn to love you, boy. If she doesn't, you just do what I told you.'

Dad's words always flood back to me when I need them most, but even more so when I don't realize that I do.

"Skylar!" I call out in a groggy tone.

I know she's here because that's one of the very few things I never had to worry about. I threatened her once with the oubliette and she never tried to go outside again without my permission. I hated doing that to her, but it made me afraid that she'd leave me and find someone else—and the only person she belongs with is me.

And Cleo, I think glumly as I get to my feet. I sway a little as I look down at my hands and see just how bruised they are.

What the fuck?

I bite my lower lip nervously for a moment, trying to remember when I've had a nightmare so goddamn vivid that it came with names and wrecked hands.

So... if it *did* happen, then how the hell did I get home?

I glance around the living room and raise an eyebrow when I see a set of cribs. Maybe I'm still in Bryden's home after all, but did he have a couch like Dad's?

I can't remember.

"Okay, it's okay," I tell myself quietly as I close my eyes tightly for a moment, then open them again.

No.

This is definitely my home. I know it because Dad's favorite recliner is sitting in the corner where he liked it to be. Even after he died, I never could find it in myself to move it. Dreams of a little boy lost, hoping for his Daddy to come home one day and make everything right again, have plagued me for as long as I can remember.

And they still do.

I know Dad's dead because I was there when he took his last breath, but some days, I wish he were still here. He would know what to do with Skylar, how to get Cleo back, and how to handle Bryden.

Though I don't believe Dad would've even flinched at seeing Cleo all grown up with a swollen belly. Unless it was his seed, he'd give even less of a fuck about her.

He would see her as a traitor, as someone who spread her legs for the first man that came along and that would have been a betrayal.

"Skylar!" I call out again, this time in a stronger voice.

Thoughts of Cleo's swollen belly explains the cribs. Maybe Skylar's finally ready to start a family. These look old enough to have belonged to us, so maybe while I was asleep she brought them out to let me know that it's time for us to continue Dad's bloodline.

But where the hell is she?

I'm irritable by the time I walk out of the living room and into the foyer. I pull open the front door to make sure she isn't outside.

My mouth goes dry as I go slack jawed at seeing Bryden's truck and their shitty sedan in the driveway next to my truck. I must have still been asleep when we got to his house... so he drove me home. It explains how I got here, but not what the fuck he's still doing here, or why he needed two extra vehicles.

I slam the door in a pure rage and turn on my heel, walking through the house, first upstairs to make sure that Dad's room is unoccupied—as it should be unless it's me and Skylar—then before I make my way back down to the main floor, I push every door open.

All the rooms upstairs are empty as they should be. I grind my teeth as I jog down the steps and check the rooms downstairs.

Empty.

Kitchen?

Empty.

Dining room?

Empty.

What the hell is going on?

Cracking my neck, I walk out of the dining room toward Dad's den and find that empty as well.

I'm confused now.

If Bryden's cars are here, then where is he? And who's with him?

Unless...

Taking a steadying breath, I walk the length of the house toward the back door. The closer I get, the more I can hear the sounds of children playing happily and it only makes me angrier.

I allowed the hope of becoming a father to corrupt my own thoughts to the point where I never would've even thought that the cribs could be for anything other than children of my own.

I wrap my hand around the back door handle, close my eyes for a moment, trying to convince myself that I'm overreacting and that when I open the door, I'll simply find Skylar playing with some of the neighborhood children that manage to find their way onto our property from time to time.

"Hey—"

But I'm wrong.

So very fucking wrong.

In the backyard of Luke Greene's home is Bryden, Casey, Xoe, and the rest of his children. The three of them are sitting in chairs watching the younger kids chase each other around in the snow-covered grass like I was so fond of doing with my sisters when we were young ourselves.

I see Skylar standing just off to the side with her arm

wrapped protectively around Cleo's shoulder, a fake smile plastered on her face and worry in her eyes.

"Hey, son!" Bryden calls out to me when I step on the back porch and let the door slam shut behind me.

I thought that by taking my sister from me he had crossed the line, but this... Dad would have *never* fucking allowed this. Dad didn't even want him, so what the fuck makes him think that he can be in this place as though it were his own without being invited in by a true Greene?

"Take her inside," I tell Skylar, balling my fists at my side.

Without hesitation, she moves quickly, leading Cleo back toward the house.

"And no matter what happens, just remember that I love you the way Dad taught me to. The only way I ever knew how," I say to her softly as she walks by me and disappears into the house.

THIRTY-ONE

Bryden

Richter is standing on the back porch, body tense as a bow string, and although Skylar listened to him about going inside with Cleo, I can see their shadows just inside the windows.

"Glad to see you're finally awake," I call out, waving him over. "Come sit with me."

"You can't be here!" he shouts, moving off the porch in a determined stride, but I just smile at him.

"You wanted your sisters here, and they are. Now we're all back home together. The entire Greene family under one roof." Looking over the house, I feel a surge of pride swelling in my chest. "Just like Luke would have wanted."

"You don't know what Dad would have wanted!" he snaps as he stops in front of me, his fists balled at his sides, practically shaking with rage.

"Seems to me like our father wanted a legacy. His blood to continue." Spreading my arms, I look around at my family who have all stopped playing to stare. "And we've done that. We can *keep* doing that, Richter. Here. Together."

"This is my fucking house, Bryden, and you're *not* a Greene. Dad got rid of you the moment he had the chance, and if you think I'm going to let you bring your fucking family here, you're fucking wrong." He takes another step closer to me and I chuckle.

"You wanted Cleo here, Richter. And if you want Cleo, you get all of us." I shrug, shaking my head a little. "I'm giving you exactly what you want, boy."

"I don't want you here! I don't want any of you here! Take your shit out of *my* house and LEAVE!" He points into the distance, and I follow his finger, running my tongue over my teeth as I brace my hands on my hips.

"No... I don't think we'll be going anywhere." The words barely leave my lips when Richter lunges, landing a punch to the edge of my jaw.

It's weak, not well-aimed, but it still sends my head to the side as the pain radiates through my teeth. He tries to follow it up, but Casey tackles him, and I let my son wrestle with Richter in the snow while I wipe my lips, feeling a grin spreading as I turn around to wave my family in.

"Everyone get inside! Richter and I need to have a talk." They all listen to me, most of them stunned into silence, but Embry is crying in Moira's arms as she carries her inside. Xoe hasn't moved though, and I look over at her, tilting my head to the door. "Go on."

"But Daddy—"

"Now, sweetheart." The tone in my voice has her eyes going wide as she nods and rushes past Casey and Richter's bodies still rolling around, trying to grapple each other.

As soon as the last kid goes through the door, I clap my hands a few times. "Okay, Casey, let him up."

"Get the fuck off me!" Richter shouts as Casey rolls to

the side and pushes himself to his feet. They're still squaring off, and I can see the rage in Casey too.

I'll teach him to control it though.

Just not today.

"Head inside, Casey. Richter and I are going to handle this."

"I'm going to fucking kill you!" Richter growls, but he's not moving yet because he's still trying to keep both me and Casey in his line of sight.

My son hesitates, but after a moment he backs away, putting space between him and Richter before he turns to head onto the porch. The door is still open, faces hovering in the doorway, and I decide it's probably a good idea for them to see what happens to people who betray their family, their blood.

It's been so long since I had to teach a lesson like this. But it's necessary.

"You really don't know what it means to be a man, Richter," I say, pulling off my coat to toss it onto one of the chairs as I chuckle, shaking my head. "Being a man means protecting your family... and you're trying to tear it apart."

"You're not my fucking family!" he shouts, lunging for me again, but I side-step him this time, making him follow me across the yard.

"All I ever wanted to do was show you what it's like to be loved," I continue, sucking my teeth clean because I can taste the copper of blood on my tongue. Probably a tooth he loosened with the punch, but I don't plan on letting him get another one in.

"I'd never love you or anyone in your bullshit family, Bryden," he growls, matching me as I take another few steps backward, leading him where I want him to go.

"Oh, I know. That's just not who you are." Smiling, I

stop moving, and he charges me. His shoulder hits hard, knocking the wind out of me, but I roll with the force of it. Hitting the snow, I shove him away and push myself to my knees so I can return the favor. My punch lands squarely on his cheek, my knuckles aching as his head cracks to the side.

"Fuck!" he curses, landing a kick in my chest to send me backward, and he's on top of me a second later. There's blood on his lips as his hands go around my throat, spit flying as he shouts, "You took my sister from me! You tried to take Skylar from me! They're *mine*! MY FAMILY!"

Choking, I grab onto his wrists, trying to pry his hands away, but he has too much leverage, and I can feel the blood pounding behind my eyes, and in a strange echo I remember what Marian's face looked like on our living room floor when I let her go.

The image sends a rush through me and I slam my knee into Richter's ribs, knocking him off balance enough to break his grip on my throat. With that first, coughing gasp, I realize I'm laughing, and I shove myself to my feet, swaying for a second as Richter stands up.

"Why the fuck are you laughing?" he growls, coming at me again, but this time I grab him, pulling him close as I wrap my arms around his back, locking him to me.

"You have no idea how alike we are, brother," I whisper against his ear, still chuckling as he tries to punch my side, but he doesn't have a good angle. Tightening my grip, I force him backward, speaking just for him and not the little audience we've drawn on the porch. "It's a shame you couldn't love your family, your own blood. I think we could have been close."

"Fuck you," he growls, and I grab a fistful of his hair, bending him back until he's off balance enough to shove to his knees. Then I lean down, putting my face right in his.

"You don't love me, Richter... and I hate to say it, but I don't think I love you either. You betrayed me, betrayed all of us, and I'm sorry to say that I don't think you're capable of loving anyone." With a sharp jerk, I slam his head into the edge of the oubliette. He's dazed, but I can still see the fire in his eyes—so I do it again. Another loud smack of flesh on stone, and he goes limp for a second, barely catching himself with a hand as I let go of him to shove the cover off the oubliette. It's heavy with snow, settled against the stones from too many years of disuse, but I put my weight behind it and it finally budges.

The yawning darkness is so familiar, the chilly air rising out of it like all the spirits of those who've died in its depths are coming up to say hi. To greet their family, ready to accept another into their ranks.

"DIE!" Richter shouts, slamming into me to grab me around the middle. With a roar, he shoves me against the oubliette, pushing me toward the open hole and I can feel the emptiness waiting below me. Flashes of Stephanie's body flicker behind my eyes, and I manage to catch the lip of the well with one hand, and Richter's throat with the other.

My fingers dig in, scratching stone on one side and squeezing off air with the other. Richter's eyes go wide, his face turning red as I twist and bend him backward over the oubliette, letting him hang there, grasping desperately at my hand, nails clawing lines in my skin as I stare into my brother's eyes. The eyes that are so much like mine, so much like Luke's.

"All you had to do was accept your fucking family, Richter. All you had to do was love your own blood, and you couldn't even fucking do that." Tightening my grip, I can see his eyes starting to roll, blood vessels popping to taint the white, and it makes me laugh again. "Like always, I have to do everything to keep this family together. *I* took care of Cleo when Luke abandoned her. *I* welcomed you into my home when you found us. I *allowed* you to see Cleo, I *let* you touch my Xoe. I did everything a good father would do. I even let Skylar see what it's like to be really loved, because you never did. And..." I sigh, another laugh escaping. "All you've done is spit in my face."

Richter convulses, his face darkening as his desperate grip on my arm weakens, and I just shake my head at the futility of always trying to make these damn kids see the truth. I should really learn to cut my losses, *before* they can do damage. Leaning in close, I make sure he can see me through whatever awareness he has left.

"Goodbye, Richter. Say hi to Stephanie for me," I whisper, and then I shove him down into the black, letting go of his throat to grab his flailing legs and send them over the edge too. There's a sickening crack just before he hits the bottom of the oubliette, and I lean over to try and find him down in the darkness, but I can't. Tilting my head, I try to listen over the sound of screaming and crying coming from the porch. There's... something. A gurgle in the depths that lets me know he's not dead yet.

More time to think.

I hear someone moving through the snow, crunching their way toward me, and I stand upright to look at Skylar. Casey is close on her heels, but where she looks numb, empty, he's got a hint of a smile on his lips.

Looks like I finally got a boy right.

"Richter?" she calls out, sounding so lost, and I back away from the oubliette so she can approach. Casey is shadowing her, hovering close, and I know he won't let anything happen to the girl.

We'll have to see if she decides to be a part of the family or not.

As I head back to the house, I see Cleo sitting on the porch, her legs half-tucked under her as she sobs, rocking back and forth while Sierra tries to soothe her. The younger kids are crying too, the sound traveling out the open door, and the older ones are all talking at once—and I can't handle the fucking noise.

"Quiet!" I snap, and most of them go silent, but Cleo is still sobbing, hiccupping as she stares at the oubliette.

Ridiculous.

"Cleo, you need to get up," I command, offering a hand down to her, but she slaps it away.

"NO! You're not my daddy!" she screams, covering her face to continue sobbing.

"I'm not your daddy?" I ask, smiling as I crouch down in front of her, and she knows me well enough to sense the danger in my tone, but she can't stop crying. Sniffling. It's disgusting and dealing with Richter wore through the last of my patience. "Answer me, Cleo. Now."

"NO! YOU LIED!" she shouts, trying to scoot away from me, but I grab her ankle in a hard grip.

"Who's your daddy then, Cleo?" I ask, chuckling a little as I wave my arm at the chaos around us. "Who?"

"Richter said—"

"Richter went in the ground, Cleo, because he didn't want to be a part of this family." Shaking my head a little, I reach over to stroke her cheek, but she tries to turn her face away and I have to grab onto her chin to make her look at me. "Are you being ungrateful, Cleo?"

"Y-you're not m-my daddy!" She sniffles again, whimpering as I dig my fingers into her jaw. "I d-don't belong with you!"

"Really?" I ask, a grin spreading over my face as I lay my other hand on her belly. "I think you do, sweetheart."

"NO!" Cleo shouts, shoving my hand off her stomach before she crosses her arms over it, like she can somehow keep me from my child. As if I would have ever let her go with Richter, to come here without me, without her *family*.

Not after everything I've done for her.

Luke left her with me.

Luke chose *me* to be her Daddy.

"I WANT RICHTER!" Cleo screams, and I switch my grip to her throat, cutting off her words as Sierra starts screaming instead.

"Richter is *gone*," I say, and then I feel someone pulling at my shoulder.

"Daddy, please. Please, she's confused!" Xoe begs, trying to stop me, and I let go of Cleo's throat just to turn and look up at Xoe, who immediately backs away. "I-I'm sorry, Daddy. I just—"

"You just *what*?" I ask, shaking my head as another chuckle rolls out of me. "Has everyone lost their goddamn mind?"

Rising to my feet, I look around at all of them. The way Sierra has wrapped her arms around Cleo, holding onto her as Cleo drags air back in. Xoe's crying too now, the girls in the doorway are wide-eyed, pale as ghosts, and Skylar is still by the oubliette. I run a hand over my face, trying to stay composed.

"What is my *one* fucking rule?" I ask, looking around at them. "Well?"

"Love everyone equally," Heather says.

"That's right!" I laugh again, grabbing my hair as I point out at the oubliette. "And Richter didn't love any of us. You all saw how he treated Xoe." Turning, I look at her, tilting my head. "Remember that?"

"Yes, Daddy," Xoe whispers, her lip trembling, and I turn my eyes down to Cleo.

"Richter didn't take care of you, he didn't love you, he didn't do *anything* for you except show up and try to take you away from your family." I chuckle again, not believing I'm even having this goddamn conversation. "And you want *him*? You want to leave our family?"

"You're n-not my daddy," Cleo blubbers, rubbing her eyes, and I feel a cold sweep of rage run through me.

"Oh, I may not have fucked your mother, Cleo, but you can bet I've been your daddy for a long time."

"No!" she shouts, looking up at me with her defiant, pouty face. "You're a liar! Richter told me, and he's my brother! My REAL brother!"

"Daddy, please..." Xoe has her hands together, tears rolling down her face, and I think she's the only one of my children above ground that has any idea what real consequences are. She's afraid, but the rest of them have had it too easy.

I created paradise for them, a beautiful, safe place for our family to flourish, to grow—but I made a mistake.

They never had to work for it. Never had to put in the blood, sweat, and tears that it takes to make a family work. To keep a family together.

And that left the door open for Richter to bring chaos into my home.

Into *my* fucking house. *My* family.

But it's okay. I can learn lessons even at my age, and I remember just how to teach them about consequences.

We can still get this family back on track.

And I'll drag all of them through it if I have to.

THIRTY-TWO

Skylar

Richter's dead.

The thought plays over and over in my mind like a horror movie on loop. He tried to protect his family the way Dad taught him to, but Bryden... he showed more signs of Dad in Richter's final moments than my brother ever did in his entire life.

Cleo's incessant crying sounds so much further away than it should as I take a tentative step off the front porch, then another and another until I'm making my way toward the oubliette. Maybe what I saw wasn't the truth, because sometimes a trauma can cause someone to see things that aren't always there. And no house holds more traumas than the one I've grown up in.

"Richter?" I call out in a voice that I don't quite recognize. The closer I get to Bryden and the oubliette, the more I feel that this might have been nothing more than a bad dream, and when I look down there... there won't be anything other than dried leaves poking out through the freshly fallen snow.

I take a deep breath and close my eyes when I'm a few

feet away from the oubliette—the place where all 'useless fucking kids' go, where all of the Greene women end up when their husbands are done with them, and I feel a bead of sweat roll down my spine. Even against the bitter cold of early winter, my body is reacting in a way that only a defiant Greene woman would.

Opening my eyes, Bryden is gone. It's just me and the hole to hell. Licking my lips, I take the last few steps toward the oubliette, drop to my knees, and grip the lips of punishment, leaning over just enough to see the inside wall. I don't want to look to the bottom yet, because even though I can hear the ragged breaths deep inside, I know that if I see him... then it's true after all.

But I know what it's like to be at the bottom of the well, and he's my brother. If there's the slightest chance that he's alive, I have to try to get him out.

I lick my lips nervously as I lean over again, this time enough to see as far down as the darkness will allow.

"Richter?" I call out again.

He doesn't answer me, not verbally anyway. Only the gentle sounds of his gurgling breaths greet me, and I can almost swear that I see the outline of his body against the snow. But... it can't be; not with the way his head is twisted.

A strangled sob escapes me, reminiscent of his breathing as I push myself back to my feet. I look around frantically for the rope ladder that Dad kept near the oubliette each and every time he would punish Mom by putting her down in the darkness, but it's nowhere to be found. That's when I remember that Richter set it on fire after the one and only time he put me in there because he said the temptation would always be there for him to do it again and he was trying so desperately to be more like Mom than Dad.

At least... until he found Cleo.

But that was before Bryden and his family.

A time when I was happier than I am now, which says a lot because that was never true happiness, but it was all we had. As long as I followed my brother's rules, he was content for the most part. The need to be a family again—a complete family—is what drove him to search for our little sister. It's what drove him to find Bryden; it's what led to the destruction of our life here.

I brush the tears away from my eyes as I lift one of my legs over the edge of the oubliette, determined to go down to my brother. Even if I can't pull him out, at the very least I know he shouldn't die alone.

"Not so fast," a voice says softly into my ear. A strong pair of arms quickly slide around my waist and pull me away from the lip, but not without a fight. I swing wildly at the person keeping me from my brother, managing to connect at least once with my fist. The familiar, now sour, scent of Casey invades my senses, causing me to reach back and grab a fistful of his hair, pulling as hard as I can—but he doesn't let go. "Skylar you have to calm down. It's okay. This is how it has to be."

"Let me go!" I scream at him as I kick my legs in the air to no avail. He's taking me farther and farther away from Richter and I can't let him die alone.

"Take her inside, son," Bryden says to Casey as he wrestles me onto the porch.

"Where do I put her?" he asks his father through harsh breaths. I pull on his hair again, turning his head to the side, but still he refuses to loosen his grip.

"The living room will do just fine. As a matter of fact, everyone go into the living room," Bryden commands in a stern tone, only waiting a second before he raises his voice to a loud shout. "FAMILY MEETING!"

His tone reminds me so much of Dad that I could almost swear it was him talking right now. And somehow, I have a feeling that even Dad wouldn't scare me as much as Bryden does in this moment.

Luke Greene used the oubliette to punish his disobedient children for the most menial things, and to dispose of his wives when they were no longer of use to him. But Bryden has said so many times that he loves and treats his family equally... and he made Richter the first Greene man to die a slow death in the oubliette.

He's taken Dad's rules and twisted them again for his own purpose and now none of us are safe.

"Come on, Cleo, we're going inside," he tells my little sister who screams at him for what seems like the hundredth time that he's not her daddy. I want to help her, but I can't get free.

Once Casey has me back inside the house—and my fist out of his hair—I lose the rest of whatever conversation his father is patiently trying to have with my little sister, but when she lets out a scream of anger and surprise, I know that he's done being patient. Dad had his limits when it came to all of his children and it seems that Bryden does too.

"Don't touch her!" I scream at him as he half-drags, half-walks her into the living room. The rest of his children look scared now—except for Casey. He has that charming smile on his face that lured me into his arms not once, but twice, and after his father shoves Cleo at him, I can almost swear that I see his chest puff up with pride.

For his father, for himself?
Who the fuck knows or cares.

The one thing I wanted for Cleo, to keep her from ever being under this roof again, I've failed at.

And as Bryden walks to the center of the living room floor, puts his hands on his hips, and surveys everyone—some crying, some scared, and only two of us angry—he shakes his head and clicks his tongue against his teeth.

"Keep her quiet," he says, nodding at Casey who quickly leans over toward Cleo and whispers something into her ear. Her sobs turn to whimpers as he rubs her stomach with his free hand, the other still firmly holding me in place next to him.

Bryden chuckles, wiping a hand over his mouth as he looks around at all of us. "Okay, kids. It's family meeting time, and we've got some important things to cover."

THIRTY-THREE

Bryden

All I've ever done is try to be a good father. It's all I've ever wanted, and I've done so much for these kids. Hell, I could have been a good father to Richter too, but he hadn't even wanted to treat me like a brother. He didn't love me or my family, and I can't figure out why everyone is fucking crying over him.

"Everyone be quiet. Now." I keep my voice even, looking around at them as they quiet down. They still sniffle, and several of my girls are wiping tears off their cheeks. Gavin and Owen are just staring at me, eyes wide, and I take a few steps to one side to see the little ones in their cribs.

Good. I have the full attention of the rest of my children. *And my sisters.*

"I know that none of you have ever had to see me put someone in the ground for betraying our family." I tilt my head to the side, glancing at my girl. "Well, except for Xoe, but all of you need to understand this—Richter betrayed us. He betrayed his own blood. He tried to tear our fucking family apart... so I don't want to hear a single one of you fucking crying over him."

"Richter wanted to save me!" Cleo shouts, and Casey shifts to grab her, covering her mouth with his hand.

"What was he going to save you from, Cleo?" I wave my hand. "Let her speak."

Casey drops his hand and Cleo pulls away from him, her face flushed, hands bunched into petite fists at her sides. "You! I lived here before you took me away! I had a mommy and a daddy, and Richter, and Skylar. This is my real family, not you!"

I chuckle, shaking my head as I ask, "Is that what Richter told you?"

"Yes! And you're a LIAR! You're not my daddy!"

"Sweetheart..." I begin, moving closer to her, but she's not smart enough to know she should move back. Though... she's never been very smart. "I didn't take you from your daddy. Your daddy brought you to me when you were five and left you with me. He chose me to be your new daddy because he didn't want you anymore."

"You're a LIAR!" she screams, and I grab a fistful of her hair, yanking her away from Sierra's clinging fingers as she whines, crying loudly again. Sierra moves forward, but it only takes a single finger pointed at my girl to stop her when she tries to reach for Cleo again.

"Stay," I tell Sierra before I bend Cleo's neck back so she has no choice but to look me in the eye. "You think I'm a liar?"

"YES!" she shouts, another snotty sniffle breaking through her crying.

"I've taken care of you. Loved you. Kept you safe, and fed, and happy for years... and *now* you think I'm a liar? *Now* I'm not your daddy, just because he said so?"

"You *are* a liar. You're not my daddy!"

"Cleo, stop!" Xoe shouts, panic laced through her voice, but one look at her shuts her up.

Grabbing Cleo's face, I look over her features. Taking note of the way they've changed since Luke first put her in my arms. So many little differences, but her round cheeks have always been there. Making her face rounder, softer, like a sweet little cherub.

But she's really a snake.

A poisonous traitor.

"You don't want me to be your daddy, Cleo?" I ask, keeping my voice gentle, and she tries to shake her head a little.

"No!" The word pops out of her lips and I smile.

"Okay then." Shoving her to the floor, I hear several of my kids shouting as I follow her down and wrap my hands around her throat.

"DADDY, NO!" Sierra screams, but I keep my eyes on Cleo's face. She's trying to pry my fingers away from her neck, eyes scrunched up tight, shoes thumping against the floor, and it's disappointing how many times I've had to do this. Betrayal shouldn't be so easy.

"You don't have to stay with us, Cleo. You can go be with Richter, and your mama, and your *real* daddy." Tightening my grip, I put more weight into my arms, feeling her muscles fighting to move air and blood past my fingers.

"Please, no," someone cries quietly, and I'm pretty sure it was Skylar, but Sierra distracts me when she drops to the floor beside us.

"STOP! DADDY STOP!" Sierra begs, both her hands wrapped around one of my arms as she pulls desperately. "Don't hurt Cleo! Please! Let her go!"

"Cleo doesn't want to be a part of this family, Sierra. I'm

just letting her go." Turning my head, I look at her. "Move back."

"No! Daddy, stop!" she cries, yanking on me harder, but in a minute it won't matter. Cleo's not even kicking anymore, her eyelids are barely fluttering. It's almost over. She's almost gone, and then I really won't be her daddy anymore. Sierra tries to throw her weight against me, but she's always been on the smaller side, and it barely shifts my hold.

Then fire erupts on my face, and I jerk back, rage flooding me. "Did you fucking scratch me?"

Sierra isn't even looking at me, she's already leaned over Cleo, shaking her, but there's no response coming from the girl I raised as my own. Grabbing a fistful of Sierra's hair, I rip her away from Cleo's body and throw her to the floor. She barely catches herself, sobbing too hard to speak as she flips to her back and shakes her head at me.

Touching my face, my fingers come away tinged with little smears of blood and I hold them out toward her. "You too, Sierra?" I can't help but chuckle as I move to her side, backhanding her with my blood-stained hand. "You want to betray this family too?"

"Cleo!" she cries, choking on her sister's name as she stares at her, pulling an arm up to try and hide her face. I immediately yank it away though, grabbing her jaw to make her look at me.

"Answer me, Sierra. Do you—"

"I HATE YOU!" she screams, and I feel my eyes go wide for a second before I backhand her again. Her cheek is bright red, but I don't give a fuck. I would never hit my kids... but Sierra doesn't love me anymore. Apparently, she loved Cleo more, and that's against the rules.

"You hate me?" I repeat, laughing as I force her to look at me again. "Really?"

"You hurt Cleo!" she shouts, sobbing harder, and I turn to look at the girl Luke left with me. The child that finally made him call me son, give me the Greene name... and then I remember the child she carries.

My child.

"Casey." I call out to him, but he already has his eyes on me, holding tight to Skylar who's practically limp in his arms.

"Yes, Daddy?"

"Go get a knife from the kitchen. Sharpest one you can find," I say, tilting my head to where Cleo lies. "You're going to save your newest brother or sister."

"NO!" Sierra screams, and I wrap my hand around her throat, squeezing until she sputters. Several of my kids moved forward, but they all freeze as I look at each of them.

"You need to do it now, Casey. Cleo deserved to go in the ground, but the child she carries is innocent." I settle my gaze on his, watching the flicker of concern leave his face just before he nods at me.

"Okay, Daddy." Turning, Casey pushes Skylar into Heather's arms, but the girl doesn't fight. She's just staring at Cleo, tears rolling, but her face is empty.

Sierra drags her nails down my arm, so much sharper than Richter's were, and she draws blood again. I hiss from the sting, looking at her again as I wrap both of my hands around her throat. "Are you fucking kidding me?" I ask, laughing bitterly. "You hate me? You want to be with Cleo? That's fine, Sierra. You can abandon us today too. Go be with your sister."

There's no sound leaving her lips anymore, but I can

feel her fighting, trying to twist away, so I shift over her, straddling her stomach so she can only kick uselessly.

"I don't know what to do, Daddy," Casey says, holding a knife as he kneels at Cleo's side. He's already lifted her sweatshirt, the swell of her belly rising high, and I try to remember everything I read. Just in case one of the kids got stuck and I had to make a choice.

But this choice is easy.

"Cut her open, low down on her stomach, but don't push the knife in too far. We don't want to hurt the baby if it's still alive."

The older kids are all silent as Casey makes the first cut, and I swear I see Cleo twitch, but the wailing of the little ones distracts me. It's like nails on a chalkboard, and I growl as I put more weight on Sierra's throat, feeling the bones grind and then there's an odd little *pop* against my palms and she stops moving. Her eyelids flutter closed, but I keep my hands where they are.

"Someone make them stop screaming," I say to the kids standing around watching Casey, and I feel my temper fraying further. "NOW!"

Brinnah and Moira jerk backward, looking at me with wide eyes before they stumble toward the cribs, softly shushing the little ones.

"I think... I think I can see it?" Casey says, and I glance down at Sierra, making sure she's gone before I let go to move to his side.

"That's it. Just carefully cut her womb open." My heart is racing as I watch his hands carefully maneuver the knife. It's incredible to see, and I'm relieved that the baby is still moving a little when Casey lifts it out.

I immediately reach over, taking my new son in my

hands to gently pat him on the back, clearing his lungs, and *his* cry is the first one I've appreciated today.

He's alive.

Something good has actually come out of this nightmare of betrayal.

Smiling, I nod at the cord. "Cut that, Casey."

With a slice, my son is in my arms, and I pull him close to my chest, wiping his face clean of the mess. "It's a boy," I announce to everyone, but no one is smiling except for me and Casey. "Are any of you going to welcome your little brother?"

"Hello, brother."

"Happy birthday."

"Welcome to the family."

None of their voices are filled with joy, and I look around at all of them as the little one in my arms squirms and cries.

"Each and every one of you need to make a decision right now about whether you want to be a part of this family or not. We've already got a few holes to dig, and if you want me to dig another... just ask." The smile hasn't left my face, and I'm sure it's because I'm holding life in my hands instead of taking it. I don't *want* to put any of my other children in the ground, but if Richter taught me anything today... it's that you have to tear out betrayal by the root. As soon as it appears.

Otherwise who knows what can happen?

"I love you, Daddy," Xoe says, her voice hushed as she bounces Embry on her hip, and it's like my girl's response unlocks the rest of them.

Each of my children repeat it, and I glance at Skylar, but she's not moving. Her eyes are still glued to the bloody mess that used to be Cleo, and I decide to be gracious. I'll let her think about it while I find something to wrap my new son in.

"I'll be right back. Why don't you kids work on cleaning this up while I take care of this little guy." Nodding at Casey, I wait for him to nod back, confirming that he'll watch them—and I know he will. He's always been a good boy, and today just proved his commitment to this family.

My memories of Luke's house are still as vibrant as ever, and my feet carry me upstairs and down the hall to his door. Opening it, I swear that for a moment I can almost smell him... but I'm sure I'm just imagining it.

The small bathroom off his room is exactly what I need to wash my son clean of his tainted mother's blood, and while I make sure the water is the right temperature... it doesn't take long for him to be perfectly clean.

And I know just what he should be wrapped in.

Stepping into the bedroom again, I open Luke's closet and run my fingers over his shirts while I bounce the babe in one arm. *This* is perfect. Simple, black cotton, and although I know it's unlikely, when I put it to my nose I'm convinced that I really can smell Luke again.

"This was your grandpa's," I tell the babe as I carefully wrap him in the shirt to keep him warm. "His name was Luke, and he started our family. He taught me what a family needs to stay together, and I promise I'll teach you too so you can carry on the Greene family legacy." My voice glides to a stop as I realize I haven't named my son yet, but I don't want to rush it.

So much has happened today, and I should wait until I can think more clearly. Usually I'd let his mother help make the decision, but that won't be possible this time. It'll just be me and him.

Looking over Luke's clothes, I wonder if any of them

could fit me. It would be a tiny way for me to feel closer to him one last time. In his home, *our* home. I'm about to shut the closet door when a small bag on the floor catches my eye and I lean down to drag it out. Moving over to the bed, I put it down and gently lay my son beside it.

"Let's see what Luke was hiding," I say to my son, smiling down at him.

When I unzip the bag, pulling the clothes out of it, I'm confused to find what *looks* like a nun costume. It's high quality though, the fabric thick, even though it seems old.

Could this have belonged to one of his wives? A keepsake?

There are some photos in the bottom, but it's no one I recognize, and the babe starts crying again before I get enough time to look at them. Shaking my head, I leave it all on the bed, *my* new bed, and pick up my son again, rocking him gently.

It's so much quieter up here. More peaceful. The boy seems to feel the same way because he stops crying, only squirming a little in the crook of my arm as I walk around Luke's bedroom.

Things have changed, been moved around, but much of it is familiar. It's the same bed. The same furniture. I run my hand along the footboard, memories clattering inside my mind, but I push them away for now.

Turning around, a frame on top of the dresser pulls my attention and I sway as I walk closer to stare into the eyes of a woman. She's smiling a little, absolutely beautiful, and I wonder if I'll ever find out who she is.

Luke had so many secrets.

So many things he didn't tell his children.

But I'm not like that. My house doesn't have secrets,

and it never will. Everything is out in the open, and we all love each other.

And anyone that tries to hurt my family will meet the same fate as anyone that has ever come up against the Greene family.

They'll go in the ground, and we'll continue on. We always will, no matter what happens. No matter who we lose.

There are just some legacies that will never die.

Epilogue

CLEO

My tummy hurts.

I'm not sure why or why it feels as faint as it does. The world around me keeps blinking in and out and it's scary.

I'm starting to feel colder, sleepier with each passing second, but no one is telling me why. I've tried asking as best as I can, but my voice won't work. I only make breathing sounds that sound like I'm blowing out air instead of making words.

I can hear the little ones crying somewhere nearby, but only barely.

Skylar's stopped screaming so I'm sure she was able to go far away from this place. She never liked it here, and neither did Richter, but when we were little, we promised each other that we'd never leave the other one behind.

Daddy took that away from us when he took me to town. He told me that I wasn't his problem anymore and that I'd be staying with family.

He told me it was my fault for not being perfect like my brother and sister, and while I didn't understand it then, being in his house again... well, I understand it now.

I wince as another wave of pain crashes over me. I struggle to put a hand on my belly, but I can't move. And while the rest of my body feels cold, my tummy feels warm.

It's the baby.

It has to be.

I close my eyes for a second then open them again and it makes my head hurt too. I know it will go away once I'm able to stand up. I'll tell Bryden that I'm sorry and he'll forgive me because he always does.

I'll take Sierra by the hand and show her the room I used to sleep in, the one my baby will sleep in, and everyone will be happy again.

"...okay?"

I try to speak and am only able to make another hissing sound. Taking in a deep breath, I imagine rubbing my tummy, hoping that it will make the baby feel better.

Bryden told me once that when the mommy gets sick, so does the baby, and I don't want that to happen.

I want to be a good mommy, like mine was. I want her to be proud of me because I know she would be happy to see me being so grown up with a baby of my own.

If you're a girl, I'll name you after my mommy. She had the most beautiful name I've ever known, I think as a tired smile creases my lips.

"...body ... holes ... now."

A high-pitched voice that sounds miles away says something I can't quite understand.

"...Casey ... dying ... sorry."

I open my eyes big and wide like Bryden taught me to do the night that he told me that he was going to put a baby inside of me. He told me that it would be his way of knowing that I was paying attention and understanding the love he was giving me.

And I need to feel that now more than anything—not *his* love, but the love of my brother and sister.

My face crumples slightly as another wave of pain crashes over me, but it's not because of my tummy and my head.

It's because he killed my big brother and I didn't have enough time to think of how to stop him.

Daddy was right.

I never was a perfect little girl and that's my fault. He gave me what he could, and Momma was so patient with me, but I... I just couldn't be what he wanted or expected.

Stupid girl, this is all your fault, I scold myself.

Maybe if I was smart like Richter or pretty like Skylar, Daddy would have loved me more. He wouldn't have hit Momma and made her cry.

A tear rolls down the side of my face, pooling in my ear as I promise the baby inside me that no matter what, I'll love it the way Momma did with me.

I'll be patient and kind.

I'll give it everything I had and more, and I'll *never* let it out of my sight because that's what good Mommas do.

And even though I know Daddy didn't love me, I still miss him being in his home again. He wasn't a nice man, but he did his best and I happened to be his worst.

"Cleo?"

I close my eyes again and smile at the faint sound of his voice.

Maybe Daddy loved me more than he was willing to admit because the colder my body gets, the more pain I feel, the better I can hear his voice.

"Cleo? Don't be afraid, okay?"

I nod as another tear rolls and the smile on my lips falters.

The pain in my tummy is going away now and so is the pain in my head.

But the biggest pain that I've ever felt—the one in my heart—it's finally starting to leave me because my Daddy is here and he's welcoming me back home.

"I love you, Daddy," I whisper as one final breath escapes me and takes all of the pain I've ever felt away with it.

THE END

About the Author

Yolanda Olson is a *USA Today* Bestselling and award-winning author. Born and raised in Bridgeport, CT where she currently resides, she usually spends her time watching her favorite channel, Investigation Discovery. Occasionally, she takes a break to write books and test the limits of her mind. Also an avid horror movie fan, she likes to incorporate dark elements into the majority of her books.

You can keep in touch with her on Facebook, Twitter, and Instagram.

More books by Yolanda:

Inferno: https://mybook.to/Inferno_
Death Blooms: http://mybook.to/deathblooms
Scavengers: http://mybook.to/scavengers

About the Author

Jennifer Bene is a *USA Today* bestselling author of dangerously sexy and deviously dark romance. From BDSM, to Suspense, Dark Romance, and Thrillers—she writes it all. Always delivering a twisty, spine-tingling journey with the promise of a happily-ever-after.

Don't miss a release! Sign up for the newsletter to get new book alerts (and a free welcome book) at: http://jenniferbene.com/newsletter

You can find her online throughout social media with username @jbeneauthor and on her website: www.jenniferbene.com

Printed in Great Britain
by Amazon